The Blood Eagle

A. L. Hatcher

A L Hatcher Author

ISBN: 979-8-9889438-0-8

EPUB ISBN: 979-8-9889438-1-5

Library of Congress Control Number: 2023915390

Book Cover by C. Rothe

Edited by: She Wrights Words, LLC

Dedication:

To my darling girl. You aren't allowed to read this
until you're sixteen, but I love you now and forever
and
To my sister, for embracing my weirdness and
always being my number one fan.

Chapter One

Tuesday, October 25th, 8:20 a.m.

The lake, smooth as glass, was covered by a thick blanket of fog that had rolled in the previous night. The woods surrounding the water stood quiet in the early morning coolness of late October, their leaves scattered at their roots in an array of oranges and reds. The weather had been unseasonably warm the past few weeks, but now the nights were getting cooler and the days shorter.

Larry Baskins inhaled a deep breath as he surveyed the placid waters of Lake Amelia. This was his favorite time of year. At eighty-two, the man didn't care much for sitting in a boat as the summer sun beat down on him, hot and unrelenting. He just didn't like to sweat and squint all day. If his old Army pals, Ben and John, came rolling into town to go fishing then Larry was in, no matter how steamy the day was. Sadly though, those days were over. Ben had moved to California to live with his daughter as he was now confined to a wheelchair, and poor John had passed away four months ago. It was his heart, they said. Just plumb gave out.

Larry sighed now, thinking of his friends. They would have loved being out on the lake this morning with him. *The rascals,* Larry thought with a grin, reminiscing of better times.

He turned back toward his battered 1991 Chevy Silverado pickup, grabbed his thermos of coffee and, with some hesitation, his cellphone. Maude, his wife of nearly sixty years, had insisted on him taking the *fandangled* contraption with him. Larry didn't really understand the excitement of having a cellphone. The way he saw it, they were nothing but trouble and a waste of time. Kids these days had no idea how to interact with others because they were so obsessed with their phones and getting "likes," *whatever the hell that meant.* No, in his day, if you wanted to talk with someone, you went to them, looked them in the eye, and talked. Or just called them, not texted, as his great grandson, Noah, called it.

Sliding the phone into the chest pocket of his flannel shirt, Larry slammed the truck door and went around to the back of the vehicle. Lowering the tailgate, he retrieved his fishing pole, tackle box, and small soft sided cooler filled with snacks and drinks that Maude had prepared for him.

God love that woman, he thought with a smile as he slung the cooler's long strap over his head and shoulder.

He slowly made it down the short trail to the old dock where he left his Jon boat moored. The dock listed to the left causing Larry's gait to become uneven as his footfalls made echoing sounds on the wooden beams. The water gently lapped around the hull of the boat as the old man bent to lower his supplies onto the dock to free up his hands. A crow cawed in the distance as Larry loaded up his boat in anticipation of the day ahead. He was hoping to catch something for dinner. Maude made the best batter to complement the filets he brought home, a true testament to the cooking skills that she had perfected over the years.

With a wobbly stance, the old man stepped gingerly into the boat, hand on the dock for support. After untying the moorings, Larry gave the dock a slight shove. He'd let the small boat drift away from the shore into deeper waters before he'd fire up the old Evinrude. Like most anglers, Larry had his "spot" that he preferred the best, the one that had provided the best fish. Now everyone had their own idea of what made their spot special but for Larry, he preferred a quiet cove toward the south end of the small lake. It was quiet, secluded, and, in Larry's mind, full of the best fish in the lake.

Lake Amelia, a small man-made body of water in rural Ohio, was barely large enough to be called a lake. It was relatively shallow, even in the springtime when rain and snowmelt made their way into its waters. As far as Larry knew, the deepest part of Amelia was only twenty feet or so. He didn't care much though. He was only there for the fishing.

Firing up the Evinrude, Larry drove the boat slowly across the lake, enjoying the crisp morning air and the warm sunlight that was starting to penetrate the dissipating fog. He took a deep breath, filling his lungs with the clean scents of nature at its finest. Pine, damp earth, algae-infused lake water—it was pure perfection to Larry. It was days like this that truly made him feel alive. Even at eighty-two, with his bones aching and vision slowly blurring, being on the lake was a refreshing respite from sitting at home in his recliner watching The Price is Right reruns while Maude chatted with her sister Nan over the latest gossip back home. He did enjoy being home with Maude, watching hours of television or doing menial home repairs, but fishing? Fishing was life.

After puttering across the small lake, Larry, enjoying the solitude the entire time, slowed the boat as he neared his special spot. No one was on the lake yet today, and if he hurried, he'd have a few hours of peace and quiet. Cutting the engine, he coasted toward the secluded cove.

He groaned inwardly when he rounded the bend in the shoreline and noticed a boat of some sort bobbing lightly on the water near his fishing spot. Larry squinted against the early morning sunlight glinting off the water as he got closer to the other boat, trying to discern what he was seeing.

Finally, once he was thirty yards or so from the other vessel, he discovered why it looked so strange. It appeared to actually be two wooden row boats stacked on one another, the upper one flipped over the bottom one. Larry shook his head at the curiousness of it all, wondering who would do such a thing. Probably teenagers playing some trick on someone, having a good laugh as they shoved someone's property out to the middle of the lake. Damn kids these days.

Skirting the shoreline, Larry drifted a little closer to the strange nautical contraption across the cove from him.

"Hello!" he called, looking around for anyone who may lay claim to the wooden monstrosity before him. He was met with silence. Raising his voice, he tried again.

"Hello! Is anyone out there? Anyone on the boat?" he called. Again, save for the gentle lapping of the water and the early warbling of songbirds in the trees, Larry was met with silence.

Concern began to churn in his stomach. Had someone fallen out of the strange boat and drowned? He didn't see anyone on the shoreline and the boat was too far away to see anyone on it. Scratching his head in consternation, Larry decided to have a closer look at the queer display before him. Instead of motoring over, he decided to use his oars and paddle over in case someone was asleep inside the row boats. He had seen people make campers out of old school buses or vans. Why couldn't someone make a floating campsite out of some old boats?

He was about twenty yards away, when the gentle October breeze shifted slightly, bringing with it a foul smell. Larry knew that odor—something was dead. A dark feeling of dread began to mix with concern and Larry felt his heart speed up. Surely it was some animal, dead in the weeds along the shore. Dipping his oar into the dark water once more, Larry propelled himself closer to the vessel.

He could hear them before he could see them. The distinct sound of flies, a fury of buzzing insects. As Larry got closer to the wooden boat bobbing before him, the fetid smell and the sound of the insects only increased. He reached up and covered his nose with one hand, while the other remained on the oar. Afraid to look, but just as afraid not to, Larry pulled even closer and nearly jumped when his Jon boat gently bumped into the wooden hull before him. The flies, swarming and angry at being disturbed, flew back toward the boat to resume their activity.

The overpowering stench of death and rot permeated the morning air and caused Larry to feel nauseated as he maneuvered his boat alongside the deserted one. It was then that he saw the true horror in front of him.

There were multiple large holes cut into the upper boat and through them, Larry was able to make out the contents. Inside, what appeared to be, human remains lay rotting, covered in flies, maggots, and other insects. Larry cried out in horror as his eyes relayed to his aged brain what he was seeing. With trembling hands, Larry reached into his breast pocket to retrieve his cell phone, subconsciously thankful of Maude's persistence.

Chapter Two

Tuesday, October 25th, 9:42 a.m.

The rain started shortly after Tess left the house. More of a mist than rain, it was just enough precipitation to cause her normally wavy dark hair to curl around her neck and face. She glanced in the rearview mirror with disdain, wishing she had brought some hairspray with her. But, as always, she was in a hurry. Adulting was a challenge sometimes, especially on days like this.

She'd been up for only a few moments that morning, groggily going through the motions: brewing coffee, letting her dog out to pee, making sure her uniform was pressed and lint-free, and her side arm, badge, and duty belt ready to go, when her cell phone buzzed. Tess paused her half-awake mutterings to glance at the bright phone screen and was instantly wide awake.

It was the sheriff. He never called patrol deputies like herself unless they needed "to talk" because something bad had happened. Everybody knew that such "talks" usually resulted in an even longer talk with Internal Affairs. A formidable man with graying temples and a paunch (from too many greasy lunch specials at Ida's on Route 72), Sheriff Burrows was said to be a kind man—once you got to know him. Tess had seen the man at the station multiple times, but as of yet, he'd spoken very little to her; and she was okay with that.

Quickly running through different scenarios in her head, Tess was at a loss as to why he'd be calling her but quickly answered.

"Deputy Dane, I need to see you as soon as possible," the sheriff asserted, nearly cutting off her greeting. "There's been an incident. I think you need to see it."

"Yes, Sir. I can be at the station in twenty minutes," Tess said, mentally calculating the time needed for her to get dressed and get over there in early morning traffic.

"Not the station. I need you out at Lake Amelia," he said abruptly.

"The lake, sir?" Tess asked, confusion wrinkling her forehead. Her normal beat was the eastern side of the county near Camden Town, not all the way out at Lake Amelia. "I–"

"Yes, the lake. They've found a body and we need you out there. And quickly, before the rain starts."

Tess's mind raced. A body? At the lake? Why would they need her? She spent most days writing speeding tickets and responding to situations involving domestic assaults, breaking and entering, and welfare checks—general patrol calls. Rarely a call involving a body. She'd seen a fair share of dead bodies in her short career, from motor vehicle accidents mostly or elderly people that were found by family members shortly after their deaths. Luckily, Camden Town, the county seat, was fairly safe and crime-free. The county alone had only had five unexpected deaths last year, only one of which was deemed suspicious.

"See you soon, Deputy Dane," the sheriff said, bringing her thoughts back to their current conversation. Before she could reply, he hung up. Tess stared at her phone for a solid sixty seconds trying to figure out what was going on, her brain and body still half asleep.

Now, as she drove down Lake Rd, toward Amelia, the misty rain had begun to increase, causing her to turn the windshield wipers on. In her hurry to get out of the house, Tess had forgotten her mug of coffee on the counter. Just thinking about the french vanilla caffeinated goodness sitting on her countertop made Tess inwardly moan. It was going to be a long day, she feared.

As she drove her patrol car down the newly paved rural road, surrounded on either side by shades of oranges and reds and trees half-naked from fallen leaves that littered the roadway, Tess tried to calm her nerves. She didn't know why she was nervous, but she was. Was it the sheriff? Was it the dead body that she was about to see? Or was it because of the mysterious circumstances by which she was asked to come to the scene?

Her phone buzzed again at another incoming call. This time it was Denny Haywood, her training partner turned investigator. She'd met Denny while still at the academy, four years ago. He'd been an instructor and then, during her probationary period as a rookie, he'd been her training partner. She had basically followed him around like a puppy in search of a treat those first few months. When she was deemed ready to patrol on her own, Tess was commissioned a vehicle and gear. Denny shortly after accepted a position with the Bureau of Criminal Investigation (BCI).

Though Denny wasn't her partner anymore, Tess still spoke with him frequently, sending texts or random photos back and forth. His daughter, Natalie (age eight going on sixteen), would even call Tess to video chat and discuss the randomness of childhood. Natalie had clung to Tess when her mother, Denny's wife of ten years, had passed away from lymphoma two years ago. *Poor kid*. Tess had tried to console the child and be there for her but felt she had failed as she herself was young, childless, and fresh out of the academy. At twenty three, she was just starting to figure out who she was.

The phone buzzed again, and Tess answered it with a grin. "Denny, how's it going?"

"Oh, you know, just usual adulting stuff," his deep disembodied voice said. "The sheriff call you yet?" he continued, cutting right to the chase.

"Yeah," Tess replied, her nervousness seeping back into her stomach. "Said I was needed at the lake."

"Best hurry. He doesn't like to be kept waiting," Denny warned. Tess could hear the wind pelting the speaker of his phone. "I'm here now, and he's already pacing."

"Oh jeesh," Tess said, gently pressing the gas and accelerating down the road. "What's this about, Denny? I can't figure out why the sheriff wants me there. I'm just a lowly deputy."

Denny could hear the stress in her voice and tried to calm her. "There's been an incident. Just relax and get here as quickly as you can. I'll explain when you get here. I gotta go." Then he disconnected the call.

A few moments later, Tess pulled her cruiser in next to Denny's black Tahoe, surveying the scene before her. The entire parking lot of Lake Amelia was crawling with police, both local and state boys. The large criminal investigation van was already parked, and crime scene technicians milled around setting up equipment while other support staff set up awnings and tables, brewed coffee and passed out doughnuts. An ambulance sat, parked haphazardly at one end of the lot, lights flashing but siren silenced.

Getting out of the car, adjusting her duty belt around her trim waist, and almost forgetting her hat, she slammed the door and went in search of the sheriff and Denny. Law enforcement was everywhere yet Tess noticed a lack of media personnel lurking about, just waiting for a top story. Knowing it was only minutes until they arrived, shoving microphones into faces and demanding answers, Tess quickened her stride into the fray.

Within moments, she found both Denny and the sheriff deep in conversation with an elderly man sitting in the back of the parked ambulance. A thick navy-blue blanket was slung around his shoulders as his thinning gray hair flapped in the gentle autumn breeze. The sky, once sunny, had turned gray and misty, bringing with it a chill. Tess watched the old man as she approached and felt a shiver down her spine.

Denny turned toward Tess as she approached and smiled, pivoting to allow her space to enter the small group that had congregated around the ambulance. Tess stood there for a moment, shivering in her black uniform, wishing she'd brought her coat. It wasn't that it was super cold out, she was just nervous and shaking, unsure why she'd been summoned. Denny must have noticed because he leaned over and whispered out of the corner of his mouth for her to relax. Tess risked a small grin and glanced up at his handsome face. He kept his face stoic and professional but she could see the sparkle of humor in his dark blue eyes.

Tess had graduated from the academy nearly four years ago at the top of her class. She prided herself on her job, being efficient and kind, yet effective, with all those she encountered, both the public and the perps. Some of the other cops told her she was "too nice" and needed to toughen up, but she truly felt that kindness went a long way. Being the daughter of a retired detective, it came as no surprise that she had followed her fathers footsteps and chosen a career in law enforcement. She rarely declined overtime, staying late to finish reports on time. As long as she was able to let out Otter, her black Labrador Retriever, and play with him for a while, she was content working on cases. Sometimes, she'd even work on her files at home while Game of Thrones played in the background as she sat cross-legged on the couch. Otter seemed to really love those times as he'd lay under her on the floor, body stretched out almost the length of the couch.

"Deputy Dane, you're here," Sheriff Burrows greeted her when he finally noticed her standing next to Denny. Tess nodded at Burrows, and then her eyes went back to the elderly man sitting in the back of the ambulance. His face was pale as he held an oxygen mask to his face and a paramedic took his vitals.

"We'll talk again soon, Mr. Baskins," the sheriff said to the old man, who barely moved in response. At the sheriff's nod, Tess and Denny followed him over toward the main incident command trailer as Tess glanced around at all the activity around them. Opening the trailer's door and gesturing for Denny and Tess to enter, he followed them inside.

The interior of the incident command post was small, somewhat cramped, yet comfortably warm and well-lit. Tables ran the length of the interior with laptop computers strewn about. A male officer Tess did not know sat at one computer furiously typing away. Maps of the county and even Lake Amelia were pinned to the wall.

"Have a seat, Deputy Dane, Denny," the sheriff said, pulling out some folding chairs. The trio sat as Tess attempted not to fidget. "Coffee?" Sheriff Burrows offered, picking up a Styrofoam cup and filling it. He held it out to Tess, and she quickly accepted. Burrows pointed to the creamer and sugar as he filled cups for himself and Denny. Tess busied herself with doctoring her coffee to taste. Trying desperately to remain calm, she wanted to scream "What is going on here?" but resisted.

Finally, after a few long moments of silence, the sheriff spoke. "So, Deputy Dane—"

"Please, call me Tess," she said, then instantly regretted interrupting him. Casting an apologetic look, she nodded for him to continue.

"So, Tess," Burrows began again. "I am sure you are wondering why you've been asked to come here this morning. I admit, this is unusual, but well... let me start at the beginning." He paused to take a sip of coffee. "This morning, we got a call about a body found in a boat. The elderly man outside, Mr. Baskins, called it in around 8:30 a.m. He was very distraught, and when we arrived on scene we found out why." Tess noticed that Burrows glanced at Denny before continuing. "The scene is quite strange to be sure, but well... it's also very disturbing... not your usual stabbing or gunshot wound. This takes on a whole new level of depravity."

"I don't follow, sir," Tess said, her face etched in confusion. The sheriff sighed, though not negatively.

"It's best if you just come with us," he said simply, his face grim.

A few moments and a short boat ride later, Tess climbed on shore, narrowly missing sinking her foot into the mud at the edge of the lake. The sheriff had explained, raising his voice over the din of the boat motor, that the parking lot where Tess had pulled in was the only official public roadway to access the lake. ATVs or boats were the only way to access the crime scene, so, choosing the latter, they had moored the boat a short distance from the scene in an effort to not disturb evidence.

"The shoreline nearest the crime scene has been processed, but please only walk on the platforms provided," the sheriff instructed, pointing to a small path formed by acrylic platforms meant to elevate foot traffic. Tess followed the sheriff, Denny behind her, toward the crime scene. Dread filled Tess with each step, unsure of what she was about to see.

Finally, a white crime scene tent came into view next to the water. Various crime scene technicians milled around, photographing and collecting, barely paying the newcomers any mind. As the sheriff approached the tent, a deputy—Greg something (Tess couldn't remember)—nodded to the sheriff and said something that Tess couldn't quite hear. She was too busy looking at the scene before her.

The tent, more of a three-sided canopy, had been erected to shield the scene from the wind and from prying eyes. It was only a matter of time before the media found out about things and began fighting for a story.

From where Tess stood, she could see an old rowboat—well, two of them—one atop the other, bobbing lightly at the lake's edge. A rope had been tied to the stern and the other end secured around a sapling. The overpowering stench of rotten flesh and the sound of flies gave indication of the boat's contents. Tess felt her stomach roil slightly as she inhaled a rather large breath of fetid air. She involuntarily covered her face with the back of her hand.

"Step back!" a technician hollered. "Lifting the lid!"

Suddenly, four men, working in tandem, lifted the second boat off the first and carried it to the shoreline. Unable to look away, Tess and Denny each took a sharp intake of breath at the sight before them.

Laying in the bottom of the second boat were the remains of a man. Naked and covered in maggots, his eyeless face lay staring up into the sky. Large chunks of skin and muscle were missing, his entrails decimated almost past identification. His face appeared to be forever in a snarl, teeth bared, as the remnants of his cheeks and lips had been eaten away by insect activity. Wispy pieces of blond hair, where the scalp was once attached, fluttered in the breeze.

It was then that Tess understood why she'd been called to this death scene. Written in light blue paint on the inside of the boat was a message. "Get Tess Dane."

Chapter Three

Tuesday, October 25th, 12:35 p.m.

"And you're sure you have no idea who that man is? Or what he wants with you?" Denny asked again. Tess sighed loudly and slapped the table.

"For the last time, NO!" Tess snapped, holding her head in her hands. "I didn't know the first time you asked, and I don't know now."

Denny sighed. They were sitting in the command trailer again, their coffee cold, getting nowhere with each other. At least Sheriff Burrows had left them alone.

"Tess, you know I trust you. Just help me understand," Denny said again quietly. "How did your name show up at a crime scene? One of the worst ones this county, if not the state, has ever seen?"

"I don't know. Honestly Denny," Tess said, feeling tears welling up behind her eyelids and willing them not to fall. "If I knew, I'd tell you. It just doesn't make any sense."

Denny sighed and sat back in his chair. His arms were crossed over his chest but the look in his eyes was one of concern and compassion. Tess stared back at him, feeling a tear break free and slide down her cheek.

"I don't know what's going on any more than you do," she said. "I don't know what happened, or what's going to happen. If they arrest me or something crazy, please promise me you'll take care of Otter—and my dad." With that the well broke, and tears started falling freely. Just the thought of her not being there for her dad made the tears fall harder. Since he'd been diagnosed with early onset dementia nearly ten years ago, Tess had been his only caretaker until around six months ago. His condition had worsened to the point she could no longer care for him at home; and he'd been moved to Tolliver Care Home in Crawley.

"Shhh," Denny said, leaning forward in his seat and taking her hand. "Don't think like that. You aren't getting arrested. We are just trying to figure out why your name was at the scene."

Just then the door opened, and Sheriff Burrows entered, bringing with him a gust of damp air. He stepped into the makeshift room and quickly looked at the two before him. Noticing the tears, he paused.

"Any progress?" He asked. Denny shook his head, causing Burrows to sigh.

Sitting down abruptly in an empty chair, the sheriff ran his fingers through his gray hair and sighed again. He eventually looked up at Tess and noticed her fidgeting again, the tears slowing.

"Look here, Deputy Dane," he started. *Oh, so we're back to formalities? Not a good sign.* Tess willed herself to stop moving. She sat up straighter in her seat and looked at the sheriff blankly.

"I'm not sure what's going on here. You're not under arrest or anything. We're just trying to figure things out, like who that guy is and why he had your name painted in his boat."

"The paint, sir," Tess said, irritated at her trembling voice.

"Yes?"

"The paint. Was there a bottle or brush in the boat? Are we even sure that the dead guy is responsible for writing that?" Tess asked, suddenly feeling defiant. She'd done nothing wrong, so why was she crying like a school kid?

"Well... no. There was nothing in the boat except the remains."

"And how did you even know that the message was there?" Tess gently challenged. "They were only just removing the second boat when we arrived," she pointed out.

"True," Burrows said, watching Tess closely. "One of the officers noticed it when he peeked through one of the holes in the top boat."

"Oh," Tess said, thinking. "So, if there was no paint bottle or brush in the boat, then the killer had to have painted it there. But why me? Why put my name there?"

"Maybe the killer thinks you know something?" Denny said, refilling his coffee cup. Reaching for her cup, he topped it off for her before returning the carafe to the coffee machine.

"Or maybe he's trying to frame her." Burrows suggested, "Like, 'Get her, she did this'."

Tess risked a glare at him. "Or maybe it's for someone else with my name?"

Denny looked at the sheriff, "Maybe the killer wants to play with Tess. Maybe he wants her included on this case for some reason we don't even know yet."

"Well, now I don't know about that." Burrows said, shaking his head. "She's a green deputy. Doesn't have the experience for something like this. Why would a killer pick her at random to work this case?"

"That's what we need to find out," Denny said. "And since I'm the lead detective on this investigation, I want Tess with me."

Tuesday, October 25th, 7:45 p.m.

Later that evening Tess was sitting on her couch with Otter at her feet, flipping through her copy of the case file. The sheriff hadn't been too happy about allowing her to work the case with the detectives. After a little bit of encouragement, he'd decided to give her a chance—just this once, because her name had appeared at the scene. And because of who her father was. Tommy Dane had been the lead detective of Swain County Sheriff's Department before his dementia forced him to retire early. Tess had a feeling that it also had to do with the fact that Denny could keep an eye on her better than when she was out on patrol. The sheriff didn't really get too much of a say anyway. With a crime scene that brutal and abnormal, BCI had been brought on board first thing.

The day had turned to night, leaving the house dark except for the soft glow of the television and a single lamp next to the couch. It was after dinnertime, but she wasn't sure how late, as she'd been so engrossed in her work. Her stomach had started growling but still she read on, writing down ideas as she went.

Suddenly, Otter sat up and ran to the front door, barking excitedly. At the same time, Tess's phone buzzed with a text from Denny. "Come to the door. Natalie has a surprise for you," it read. A grin appeared on Tess's face as she hopped up and went to open the door.

"Tess! Otter! We brought pizza!" Natalie announced as she ran through the door and into Tess's arms. Otter danced around, tail wagging, waiting on Denny to put the pizza down and pet him. Denny knew the routine at this point: empty your hands and play with Otter or else he'll go crazy.

"Hi, guys!" Tess said, suddenly realizing how lonely and quiet the house had been. "What a great surprise! Come in, come in." She took the hot pizza box from Denny's hands and watched as he immediately began petting Otter, making funny voices that the dog seemed to like. Otter started whining and barking, long pink tongue hanging out of his mouth.

"I thought you could use a break," Denny said, casting a glance at the casefile strewn about on the couch. Tess gave him an appreciative look, then went to quickly shove the papers and crime scene photos into the file to keep Natalie from seeing them.

"Thank you," she told Denny as she followed him into her small kitchen, which sat just off the living room. She could hear Natalie talking to Otter in the living room. The hallway filled with the sounds of the young girl throwing Otter's tennis ball and the dog scrambling after it.

"I've been reading the report so far, which isn't much," Tess said, gathering plates and napkins and setting them on the counter. "Have they ID'd the man yet? Maybe that will help figure out how my name got on the boat?"

"No ID yet," Denny said, finding cans of soda in the refrigerator and popping the lid on one. He offered another one to Tess, but she declined with a shake of her head.

"I don't drink that stuff. I keep it in there for you and Natalie," she gave him a small grin. Denny smiled and took a long gulp from the can.

"The body is with the medical examiner now. They will be doing the autopsy and will send the report over as soon as possible. Hopefully they will be able to positively get a name for the poor guy."

"Sheriff wants me there at eight in the morning for the progress briefing. I'm not sure what I can really offer the team though," Tess said, feeling a wave of apprehension again. Why was her name on the boat? She sighed as she put some pizza on a plate for Natalie and sat it at the small table near the kitchen windows.

"Hey, don't stress. We'll get through this. We'll find out all the information we can and hopefully catch the bastard who did this," Denny said, placing a gentle hand on her shoulder. "I don't know what to expect either, and I'd be freaking out if my name randomly showed up at a crime scene too. I get it. But you've done nothing wrong, so the connection has to be from somewhere else. Maybe once we get an official ID, we will be able to connect the dots better."

Chapter Four

Wednesday, October 26th, 8:04 a.m.

The briefing started a few minutes after eight the next morning. Tess had been there since 7:30, drinking coffee while glancing at the notes she'd made the night before. She nervously reached up and messed with her long brown hair, pulling it into a ponytail. Normally, when out on patrol, she'd have her hair pulled back in a low bun to keep it out of her way. Today though, out of uniform and wearing dark dress slacks and a blue button-down shirt matching her eyes, she'd decided to wear her hair more casual.

Waiting for the meeting to start, Tess glanced around at her surroundings. There were seats sitting around a large meeting table in the middle of the room. Toward the back of the room sat a small, wooden table holding a box of Jolly Pirate doughnuts and a woven basket full of bananas and apples. On the other side of the doughnuts was an old, yet functioning, coffee pot that burbled as it brewed yet another carafe of mediocre coffee.

As she sat at the conference table, papers and notes tidy before her, Tess watched as the room began filling with officers. She knew some of them, local detectives she'd worked with previously. Some of them she'd only seen yesterday at the crime scene. State boys probably. She listened to them talking in hushed tones, some glancing at her on the sly. She felt like she was on center stage somewhere, all eyes on her, and she didn't like it one bit.

She wondered what they were thinking of her and saying behind her back. Being one of the few female officers on the force was hard at times, trying to fit in with the "boys club." She'd grown thick skin early on, but this situation was new. Her name had appeared at a crime scene, and a grisly one at that. Fighting the urge to flee the conference room to get away from their stares and hushed whispers, Tess scrolled on her phone as though she was looking for something. In reality, she was just keeping a low profile as best she could.

"Dude, you guys remember the jumper from over in Crawley during the spring?" came a loud voice from the doorway. Tess glanced up and saw Ricky Osbourne, one of the more senior deputies whom she'd had the unfortunate opportunity to work with from time to time. He was loud and crass and had asked her out on numerous occasions. She'd declined his offer each time and tried to avoid him as best she could. Now, as he stood in the open doorway, Tess groaned inwardly.

"Yeah. What of it?" Detective Malone said from his seat nearest the doughnut table.

"They finally got the tox report back. That chick was on everything–heroine, meth, fentanyl—you name it," Ricky said, as he came into the room to help himself to a doughnut. "Everybody knows she was prostituting in both Camden Town and Crawley. Doesn't surprise me one bit. I'd jump too."

"Hey Osbourne, you're an ass," Malone said with a smirk. "What was her name again? Marge? Mary? She had a mental illness, man. Cut her some slack."

"Whatever, man," Ricky said, ignoring his radio when it blared to life. His mouth was full of doughnut when he finally caught sight of Tess, who was trying hard not to be noticed.

"Hey Tess, what are you doing here, hanging out with these losers?" he smirked, walking up to her and standing way too close for comfort. Tess had to crane her neck to even look up at him.

"I'm here for the briefing," she said politely, noticing a chunk of custard on Ricky's face. She quickly looked away.

"Oh, so are you going for detective now?" He asked, cramming another mouthful of doughnut into his mouth and chewing loudly. "I don't know why you'd want to hang out with these asshats when you could hang out on patrol like me."

The guys around the table started laughing and rolling their eyes at that. Tess, wanting to be anywhere but there, gave a small laugh. She rolled her eyes and went back to scrolling her phone, dismissing him.

"Osbourne, you're only jealous because you've been on patrol for like, what... twenty five years? And you keep failing the sergeant's exam!" Denny said as he came into the room and took a seat next to Tess. Tess instantly felt more at ease, having Denny by her side.

"Whatever, Haywood," Ricky said, childishly glaring at Denny before grabbing a second doughnut as he headed for the exit, nearly bumping into the sheriff. Getting a slight scowl from Sheriff Burrows, Ricky tucked his tail and skirted around him, heading down the hall.

"Alright gentlemen," the sheriff said, taking his place at the head of the table. Catching Tess's eye, he added, "and ladies. Let's get to work. We have a killer to catch, and the media is already having a field day." He sat down brusquely, laying a stack of papers and reports in front of him. "Let's start by going around the table, sharing any info we've gathered so far. Any word yet about a proper ID for the victim?" he glanced around the table.

"If I may sir..." one of the state officers started.

"Yes, Officer...?" The sheriff said, looking over at the redheaded officer who had spoken.

"Claybourne, sir. Aaron Clayborne, BCI," the officer said completing the sheriff's sentence. After a nod from the sheriff to proceed, Claybourne opened the file in front of him. "The man from the boat matches the description of a missing person from Crawley: Gary Hinsley, aged 42. He's a father of two boys, married to wife Sarah for ten years. He works as a mechanic off of Route 72, at a shop called 'Rusty's Muffler Shop and Repairs'."

Claybourne stood then, pacing toward the markerboard at the far end of the conference room. He picked up a black dry erase marker and wrote out the potential victim's information. The marker made irritating squeaking sounds as it moved across the board. Claybourne then recapped the marker and, grabbing some tape and a piece of paper from his folder, taped it to the marker board. The paper had a photo on it, most likely from a driver's license, of a middle-aged man with medium length blond hair and piercing blue eyes. Tess couldn't place the man or his name. He was a stranger to her. She wrote the name down on her notes, vowing to research him later tonight, desperate to find the connection between him and herself.

"As far as we know now, the victim is tentatively identified as Gary Hinsley, based on the missing persons' report while we await the ME's report and dental records to be processed. Considering the state of the body, the wife has not been asked to make an ID," Claybourne continued. "She has been informed about the investigation so far as I'm sure the media will be out in force. As always, this man's name is to be left out of the papers until the final reports are in." With that, Claybourne went back to his seat and sat down.

The sheriff nodded at Claybourne and then said, "Alright, anyone else? Any information about the boats? Any witnesses so far? There's no official surveillance at the lake but did anyone from the nearby houses see or hear anything? These are the questions we need answered."

"Mike Seawell, forensic investigator from BCI," said a dark-haired man with round wire-rimmed glasses, as a way of introducing himself. "We are working on analyzing some red fibers found near the scene, caught in the weeds at the shoreline. May be nothing of importance or could be super helpful. It's just too early to say." Mike hopped up then, a photo in hand, and made his way toward the markerboard. He taped a picture of the red fibers caught in the weeds. Next to it, he hung a photo of a partial boot print.

"This shoe impression was found near the boat's mooring. Although the mud in that area was mostly dry at the time of the investigation, the impression is fairly deep, indicating that the print was made when the ground was rather soft. Assuming the ground was soft due to rain, that would indicate it was made sometime early last week when we had that storm. The drizzle yesterday morning was not enough to soften the ground to the point of making such a deep print. My team took plaster casts of the impression and are currently at work determining size and brand. As you can see from the photo, it was only a partial print."

"Good work, Seawell," the sheriff said, jotting down some notes. "Ok, any information about the boats?" he said looking around.

"We've looked them over and they seem like generic wooden fishing boats. They are older models, not new by any means," Officer Malone said, speaking up. "The wood seems weathered, like they've been sitting out in the sun for a while, out of the water."

"How can you tell that?" Denny asked, taking a sip of coffee. Malone looked at Denny and nodded.

"Because of the bleaching of the wooden hull. The exterior, the part that would be touching the water, was bleached out on both boats, weathered and splintering due to the elements. The interior, though soiled from the body, appeared polished and smooth still. The wood on the inside appeared to have been sheltered from the elements. It's almost as though the boats were stored upside down, outside in a sunny or unprotected area. The bottom one also appeared to have been recently re-caulked. Otherwise it would have sunk under the weight of the body and the second boat."

"What about the holes cut in the top boat?" the sheriff asked.

"The holes appear to have been made with a saw or some tool like that, not smashed into it with a hammer. The edges of the holes have minute ridges from the saw's blade. I have photos taken by the forensic team if needed. But basically, it looks as though someone deliberately made the holes for some unknown reason," Malone said.

"But why two boats...?" the sheriff wondered out loud.

Just then the door opened to the conference room and a tall, thin woman with long dark hair rushed in, files in her arms and a coffee cup in her hand.

"Sorry I'm late. It was a long night and traffic this morning...Yikes!" she said, giving the sheriff an apologetic smile.

"It's okay, Abby. This time," the sheriff said, although he didn't seem too upset. "Everyone, for those of you that don't know, this is Abby Summers, the medical examiner. She's worked a late night for us, so please cut her some slack."

Abby smiled at those gathered around the table and adjusted her yellow blouse. With a stressed-out sigh, she took a sip of coffee.

"So, Dr. Summers," the sheriff said after Abby got settled. "What do you have to report?" All questions about the boats were instantly forgotten.

"Well sir, I was able to do a cursory external exam last night. I'll be conducting the internal exam later this morning." Sliding on a pair of dark framed glasses, she opened her files and began. "The victim is male, 6 feet 3 inches tall, one hundred and... well... forty pounds, although most likely heavier in life."

"Come again?" Claybourne asked, leaning forward with a confused look on his face.

"Well, you see, there were rather large... chunks... of him missing," Abby said. "There appear to be slashes or cuts made across both thighs, calves, and arms. Chunks of flesh removed. Because of decomposition and insect desecration, along with the missing pieces of flesh, the poor man is most likely lighter now than he was when he was alive."

"One hell of a weight loss plan," someone muttered, causing a scowl to appear on the sheriff's face.

"Anything else of note?"

"Yes," Abby said, referring to her notes. "The man was naked when he was placed in the boats. He was also covered with a sticky substance. I'm pretty sure it was… honey? I've sent samples to the lab to confirm. It was hard to determine by smell because, well, decomp. But it appeared that the man had been covered with it for some reason. There was also fecal matter all over his inner thighs and rear end. Almost like he'd laid in his own waste for a while."

Suddenly Tess felt ill and her face blanched. She must have leaned toward Denny because she suddenly felt his hands on her shoulder and knee.

"What's wrong? Are you ok?" he asked. Tess felt all eyes in the room on her and she swallowed hard before glancing up at the sheriff. He was staring right at her, squinting as though he suspected she was guilty of something.

"Deputy Dane, are you alright?" he asked.

"Yes, Sir." Tess said, cringing at the shakiness in her voice. "It's just…" She turned and looked at Abby, at the woman's kind eyes watching her. "I think he was tortured."

Chapter Five

Wednesday, October 26th, 8:42 a.m

"What do you mean, tortured?" Abby said, watching Tess's pale face.

"Well... uh," Tess began, "last night when I got home I started researching boats, and what two boats mean, if anything. And I came across something." She paused, glancing at Denny and then back to the ME, avoiding the sheriff's steely gaze.

"There used to be a torture practice called "The Boats." It's also called scaphism. It's allegedly an old Persian way of executing people," Tess paused, opening her file to read from her notes. "They would basically lay the person naked in a boat, sometimes making their legs and arms hang out, and then they'd force them to eat a mixture of milk and honey. They'd even pour it on their faces. Poked their eyes out. The flies and bugs would come and start eating the body while the person was still alive. The victim would lay in their own waste and the insects would enter any orifice they could find. Dying this way could take days. I read one report of a guy who lasted seventeen days before he finally died."

Tess handed Abby some printouts of website stories she'd read the night before. Abby took them and perused the contents.

"Dear God..." Abby said, covering her mouth as she read.

"That's disgusting," Malone said, "Who could do that to someone?"

"It doesn't match exactly, but I think you're on the right trail," Denny said, reading over Tess's shoulders. "Our guy didn't have his arms and legs sticking out, for one."

"But they were tied behind his back," Abby said, glancing over at him. "The chunks of missing flesh don't quite fit either, unless it was meant to hurry the process along."

"Maybe it's torture for revenge? You know, getting your pound of flesh?" Denny said. Sheriff Burrows nodded in agreement. Seawell, the forensic investigator, looked ill. Tess just sat there, confused by the killer's perceived connection to her, and by how she'd gotten involved in such a vile thing. She felt like she might vomit.

"Good work, Dane," Burrows approved, looking toward Tess. She just nodded and looked back at the ME.

"Were you able to find out anything else?" Tess asked.

Abby nodded. "There was a tattoo on the man's left pectoral area that was visible once the body was washed. Looked like a phoenix with something in its claws. The skin was missing and so it's hard to determine what the bottom of the bird looked like. Here." She produced a printout photo of a close-up view of the tattoo and passed it around the room.

The bird definitely looked like a phoenix, with flames of oranges, reds, and yellows. Tess couldn't figure out what was in the bird's claws either, due to the tearing of flesh made by the post-mortem insect activity.

"We need to follow up on all these leads," Denny said. "Seawell, you follow up on the foot impressions and fibers. Claybourne, you work on finding out where the boats came from. Check local marinas, boat repair and retail shops, local woodworkers with a history of boat making, that type of thing. Abby, I'm sure you'll report back once you've done your internal examination and received the tox reports. Dane and I will go talk to the wife; show her the tattoo and interview her. The family liaison officer is there now providing aid. I'll get Miles and Scafferty to make the rounds at the neighboring houses near the crime scene, to see if anybody heard or saw anything."

Tess knew Deputies Miles and Scafferty. They were good officers, always polite to her and had a good eye for detail. They had been partnered up for a while now, both studying for the detective exam. Though they were technically patrol officers, they were the two that the sheriff called on when they needed extra hands for a case. Their thoroughness and passion for the job were evident. Tess hoped to one day be where they were, studying for her own exam.

"Everyone, be back here at six sharp this evening for a short debriefing. Thank you. And good luck out there."

Wednesday, October 26th, 9:25 a.m.

"So, what do we have so far?" Tess thought aloud as she and Denny raced down Route 72, headed toward the house once lived in by Gary Hinsley. They had called ahead and let Mrs. Hinsley and the liaison officer know they were en route. "We have a mechanic, married with children, who was tortured and killed. But why? Once we figure that out, then maybe we'll figure out why I got roped into this mess."

"True," Denny said as he guided his Tahoe around a curve in the road. The day was sunny, the sky blue. "I hope we get some good intel from the wife." Silence filled the car, both of them lost in their own thoughts. After a moment, he turned to Tess, watching her from behind the lenses of his aviator sunglasses.

"That was great work back there. All that stuff about torture. You're really taking this job seriously. I always knew you'd make a great cop, from the first class at the Academy."

"You did not," Tess laughed, suddenly embarrassed from the sudden praise, yet pleased by it. "But thank you. I try."

"It shows," Denny said, turning his eyes back to the road. "You always worked hard in class, always got straight A's. Some of those other cadets didn't have a chance with you around."

Tess jokingly punched him in the arm, laughing, "That's not even true. Maybe they should have worked harder. You're lucky you got stuck with me as your rookie training partner."

"There was no luck involved with that." He said quietly, eyes still on the road. Tess's laughter quieted abruptly, and she watched his profile closely.

"Wait...does that mean you–" but her question was cut off as his cell phone trilled.

"Haywood." He said as he pressed the Bluetooth button to connect the phone to the car's speakers.

"Hey, Daddy." Natalie's small voice filled the vehicle.

"Hey Baby, what's up? Shouldn't you be in class right now?" Denny said, glancing at the digital clock on the dashboard.

"Yeah," Natalie said. Tess thought she sounded like she was sniffling but couldn't be sure. Her mind was still reeling from Denny's near admission to personally requesting her as a rookie. Had she really heard him correctly?

"What's wrong Natalie? Are you crying? Where are you?" Denny asked, his voice filled with concern.

"I'm in the girls' bathroom. I told Mrs. Hall I needed to go potty, but I really didn't," came the child's response, along with another sniffle.

"Okay... but why are you in the bathroom crying?" he asked. Tess knew he'd given Natalie a cell phone for emergencies, one of the cell phone styles made for children. The phone called four people of the parents' choosing. All the parent had to do was enter the chosen contacts—grandparents, neighbors, whoever—into the phone, and it gave the child the ability to call them. But this type of phone did not have internet access or free range of a real cell phone. It was perfect for times like this.

"Lainey Garrett is saying nasty things about me again, and I can't take it," Natalie said, her voice becoming muffled as she started sobbing. "Mean things about Mom."

Denny tightened his grip on the steering wheel. A muscle in his jaw began to twitch as he ground his molars together.

"I'm sorry, Natalie," he sighed. "I thought things had gotten better with her. I'll talk with Mrs. Hall again. I'll even bring Principal Jeffers in on it this time. This needs to stop."

"Can you come get me?" Natalie asked, her voice small and pleading. "Please?"

"I'm on my way to talk with someone, sweetie. It's very important and I can't leave at the moment," Denny said, a look of parental guilt etched into his face. "I'll come as soon as I can. Try to go back to class and ignore Lainey if you can. If that's too hard, go to the nurses station. I'll call the school and let them know what's going on. Can you try to go to class again?"

A loud sniff. "I can try, Daddy. I'll be strong."

Denny smiled, though she couldn't see him. "That's right, Natalie. You're very strong. I'll see you as soon as I can. I love you."

"Love you too, Daddy." And with that, Natalie ended the call.

Denny sighed. He glanced at Tess, a sad look on his face. "Sorry about that."

"It's ok," Tess said. "I want to punch Lainey, whoever she is. How could someone be mean to Nat? She's the sweetest thing ever!"

"Lainey Garrett. She's been a pain in the ass since kindergarten." Denny said, running his hand through his thick dark hair. "She's been after Natalie since day one, even before Cassie died. She'd make mean comments on Natalie's hair, clothes, lunch, whatever, just trying to embarrass her or start fights."

Tess so rarely heard about Denny's dead wife, Cassie, and their life before she got sick, that Tess was unsure what to say. She felt so sorry for Natalie, being bullied at school and having to grow up without a mother. She knew what it was like growing up without a mom around, but technically, Tess's mother was still alive. She was just too selfish to be a part of her daughter's life.

Denny checked the GPS, "We should be at the Hinsleys in about fifteen minutes. I'm going to call the school, get an appointment with Mrs. Hall and the principal. This needs to stop." Tess tried to half listen as Denny called the elementary school and explained, yet again, what was going on between the two girls. Tess was surprised how polite, yet direct and even-tempered, Denny was as he discussed the matter with the school. Tess felt like if she were in his shoes she wouldn't have been so nice.

Chapter Six

Wednesday, October 26th, 10:06 a.m.

As predicted, fifteen minutes later Denny was pulling up outside the Hinsley residence. A small house in an older neighborhood, the property looked well-maintained, the grass freshly cut. Even the leaves had been raked into neat piles, ready to be bagged up. He noticed that the media were already starting to swarm and he let out a small groan.

Cutting the engine, he grabbed his cell phone and gave Tess an "are you ready for this?" look. She gave him a slight nod, and the two got out, slamming their doors lightly. They quickly made their way up the driveway, ignoring the onslaught of media questions assaulting them.

The front door, painted yellow with a wreath of fall leaves in its center, opened before Denny could even knock. Officer Diane Kennedy, the family liaison, ushered Tess and Denny inside and swiftly closed the door.

Instantly silence filled the air, the noise and verbal chaos from the media storm outside becoming a soft drone.

"Officers," Kennedy greeted them with a nod. "We've been expecting you."

"We came as soon as the morning incident meeting was over. How are they doing?" Denny asked quietly, looking around for Mrs. Hinsley or the children. The house was quiet and dark, as though a cloud had settled over it.

While Kennedy and Denny quietly talked, Tess silently glanced around, taking in her surroundings. She was trying to discern what kind of family lived here. Who were the Hinsleys? Were they a loving, close-knit family? Or rather one that was cold and distant with one another?

They stood in the foyer of the small house. The walls were painted a light gray, and the trim white. Small black metal hooks on the wall held an assortment of seasonal jackets, two of which were child-sized, along with two small backpacks. Shoved haphazardly under a narrow white bench, shoes and an array of brightly colored, mud-spattered rubber boots lay forgotten.

A few framed photos of a smiling family lined the walls, leading from the foyer and up a flight of stairs. Standing close to one of the photos, Tess looked closely at the family, arranged nicely on a plaid blanket, a pond or lake in the background. Lake Amelia, possibly, as it was a popular place for photography. Leaves, in hues of oranges and reds, lay scattered about the family as they sat smiling for the camera. Was it taken last fall? How sad that just a year or so later, the smiling man in the picture would be found dead, floating in a boat, as insects scavenged his body.

"That was at Lake Amelia," came a voice from behind Tess, causing her to jump. She whirled around to find the woman in the photograph, Sarah Hinsley, eyes red and swollen from crying, standing behind her at the base of the stairs.

"You have a beautiful family," Tess said. "Are the boys twins?" She pointed to the family portrait, at the two blond-haired boys smiling back at her.

"Yes. Garrett and Gavin," Sarah said, a small smile crossing her sad face. "They are six. They're with their grandmother right now. I sent them there while I spoke with you about Gary..." Her voice started to break when she said her husband's name and she trailed off, turning into the living room, away from the smiling faces on the wall—of the family they had once been.

Officer Kennedy nodded toward Tess as she led them into the living room after Sarah Hinsley. They found the woman sitting at the edge of the couch, as though she may bolt at any moment. A wad of tissues in her hand, she looked like she would crumble at the littlest provocation.

"Mrs. Hinsley, this is Detective Denny Haywood and his partner, Deputy Tess Dane," Officer Kennedy began. Denny and Tess sat where indicated: Denny in an armchair and Tess at the opposite end of the couch Sarah Hinsley occupied. "They are here to ask you some questions about Gary so they can find out what happened to him," Kennedy said, a gentle hand on Sarah's shoulder. After Sarah gave a small nod and a sniffle in acknowledgement, Officer Kennedy stepped out of the room. Tess was pretty sure the officer was eavesdropping around the corner, out of sight.

"I'm sorry to meet under these circumstances, Mrs. Hinsley—" Denny started.

"Please. Call me Sarah," the woman said, turning on the couch to better face him. Denny gave her a sympathetic smile and nodded.

"So, Sarah, as you know, we are here to learn more about your husband, about his life—any trouble he might have had, enemies," Denny said, watching the small woman in front of him closely. "We are trying to find the person or persons who did this to him."

Sarah nodded, staring at the floor. Her shoulder-length brown hair covered her face from view, but Tess could see her shoulder heave as she cried silently. Dabbing at her eyes, she slowly looked up at Denny with large blue eyes. She gave him the slightest nod to continue.

"Let's start at the beginning, shall we?" Denny said. "When did you first meet your husband?"

"I was in college, senior year," Sarah said, dabbing her eyes again while sniffling. "I was in finance, and he was in trade school for auto mechanics. I was waiting in line at Starbucks for my coffee when he walked in and stood in line behind me, all greasy and dirty from working on cars all day," she smiled slightly at the memory. "I don't remember what was said, but he started making small talk with another customer and before I knew it, he'd included me in the conversation. Well, the other person eventually left, and I got my coffee. I had just made it to a seat, gotten my laptop out, when the guy came up to me. He introduced himself as Gary, and we started talking again: not about anything in particular, just random stuff. Before I knew it, he was sitting across from me, our coffee was cold, and my term paper hadn't written itself. I do remember having to stay up until after midnight that night writing the dumb thing because I'd gotten home late. You see, after we sat at Starbucks for three hours—*three hours! Who does that?*—we went on a walk around town, chatting the evening away. We ended up having dinner together that night... some chicken place that's out of business now. Anyway, we swapped numbers and before we went our separate ways, I'd agreed to go out with him the next evening. We were married two years later."

"And how would you say your marriage was? Loving? Rocky?" Denny asked, jotting something in his notebook. Tess cast a glance at his lap, trying to see what he was writing. When Sarah began speaking again, Tess looked back up at her, watching her as another tear coursed its way down her cheek.

"Like any other marriage of ten years, I'd guess," Sarah said, dabbing at her nose again. "We loved each other. Sure, we fought occasionally like all couples do—mostly over money or his drinking. For the most part, things were fine. Good. I didn't have any complaints, especially now that he was finally getting some help with the alcohol. He was sober eighteen months this past month." She smiled then, a sigh escaping her lips. She pushed her hair behind her ear and pressed on. "And no, before you ask, I wasn't cheating on him, and he wasn't cheating on me. I know when someone dies unexpectedly the partner or spouse is always the first suspect. I already answered so many questions yesterday." She paused then, rubbing her forehead. "I'm sorry. My head is pounding, and I feel almost nauseous. It's just all too much."

"I'm sorry, Mrs. Hinsley... Sarah. I know this is frustrating. The officers who spoke with you yesterday were just trying to establish a baseline for inquiry. Deputy Dane and I are here to ask some follow up questions, get to know Gary, the state of your marriage, and his job. Please bear with us. We are only asking these questions so that we can work together to find the person who did this to your husband."

Sarah nodded, balling up her tissue in her hand. She glanced from Denny to Tess, then back again when Denny began to speak.

"Tell us about Gary. His personality, his goals. Did he have a lot of friends? Enemies?"

"He was....Gary," Sarah began, picking up a framed photo off the end table next to her. She gazed down at it, the photo portraying the young couple on their wedding day, so full of hope and promise. "He was a joker. Always out to make people laugh. He was the life of the party. He partied a lot back before the kids were born." She paused, thinking for a moment. "The drunker he got, the crazier he got. Loud, sometimes pushy. I remember one night, before kids, when he came home much later than normal. I came downstairs to find him stumbling around in the dark, drunk out of his mind. When I flipped on the kitchen light, he got pissed at me. Started squinting at the light, yelling. And then..." Sarah paused again, almost as though she was afraid to go on. With resolve she continued, "He came at me fast. I froze, waiting for him to hit me or kick me. Something. But instead, he started getting physical." She turned then, her eyes large.

"He attacked you? Sexually?" Denny prodded gently. Sarah started to nod but then shrugged instead.

"I mean, we were married, so it wasn't *that* wrong... right? Like, I told him to leave me alone because he was drunk. I even shoved him off of me and went back to bed. I thought he'd changed his mind, or maybe even just decided to sleep on the couch that night. I was almost asleep when he barged in and started to tell me it was his right to do with me what he wanted because he was my husband. I told him that was bullshit and if he even thought about touching me like that again, I'd call the cops and divorce him so fast. He just looked at me and then puked all over the rug and our bed comforter," Sarah frowned.

Then she continued, "The next morning, while he was stuck with a raging hangover, I told him he better not ever come home drunk like that again. I told him that I wasn't his possession to do whatever he wanted to with. He ended up just drinking at the bars then, sleeping on friends' couches. It wasn't until almost two years ago that he was finally in a place to get help. He was coming home late one snowy night, and the roads were slick. He'd been drinking and lost control of the car. He crashed it into a guardrail out on Quaker Hollow Road, almost killing himself. It was that accident that caused him to realize that he needed to change: for himself, and for Gavin and Garrett. He started at AA; never missed a meeting; followed the steps. If you ask me, I'm glad he wrecked that car. It was the wake up call he needed. He never knew how close I was to leaving with the boys. I was done with my marriage, done with worrying about him all the time. But AA saved him and our marriage. Our bond has been the strongest it's ever been." Lost in thought, Sarah started crying again, tears streaming down her face.

"Did Gary have any enemies?" Denny inquired. Sarah shook her head, thinking.

"No," she said, "none that I know of anyway. He was a likable person, except when he drank."

"Where did he attend the AA meetings?"

"Down at St. Catherines, that old church on Poplar Street," Sarah said. "Every Thursday evening at seven." She watched as Denny made notes.

"Any trouble on the job? Any irate customers? Friction with coworkers?"

"Not that I know of; nothing he mentioned to me at least," Sarah said, mindlessly picking at her cuticle.

"Any friends he hung out with?"

"Just Cody and Justin, mainly," Sarah said. "Cody lives a few doors down. He and Gary bonded over their love of grilling and old cars. Justin is a childhood friend that lived across town until about six months ago. He got a job transfer to Japan, of all places."

"When was the last time you saw Gary?" Denny asked. Tess perked up at this question. She'd already heard from the ME and crime technicians that Gary had probably been killed a few days prior to being found based on decomposition, although those were just preliminary opinions.

"Today's what? Wednesday?" Sarah said, thinking back. "I would have to say last Thursday night, when he left for his meeting."

"You hadn't seen your husband since Thursday and didn't think that was suspicious?" Tess asked, instantly wishing she could reel her words back in. She was there to watch, listen, and take notes. It was Denny who was conducting the interview.

Sarah looked at her, apparently taking offense with Tess's tone. "No, Deputy Dane, I didn't think it was suspicious. I was out of town. I left last Monday and came back early yesterday morning. I'd only been home a couple of hours before the cops came and told me about Gary."

"Why were you out of town?" Denny asked, ignoring Tess's interruption.

"My mother had knee surgery a couple of weeks ago. I've been going back and forth, trying to help out. This time, I took the boys with me and just stayed there for a few days. I talked to Gary a few times while I was gone. But the last time I heard from him was Thursday night, right before his meeting."

"I thought you said you saw your husband last Thursday. Just now, you said you talked to him. Which was it?" Denny asked, referring to his previous notes. Sarah seemed flustered.

"Well, actually, it was a text," she said, "I sent him a text, telling him I was thinking about him, and not to work too hard. He'd been working late all week and hadn't been good about calling me back. I usually get a late-night text."

Denny jotted down some notes, flipped pages back and forth for a moment. "So, the last time you actually saw your husband, alive and in the flesh was...?"

"A week ago Monday, on my way out of town," Sarah said, rubbing her forehead again. "I had picked the boys up from school and we stopped by Gary's work to say goodbye before heading out. We even took him some fast food for dinner because he was going to be working late."

"And how did Gary seem when you saw him?"

"Normal. He seemed tired, but happy to see us. He was covered in grease with car parts spread out everywhere; just a typical Monday at the shop."

They asked a few more questions to set a baseline for Gary's whereabouts and normal routine when Tess noticed that Sarah seemed to be getting very exhausted. Denny must have noticed too, as he abruptly closed his notebook, effectively ending the interview.

"Ok," Denny said, "that's about all the questions I have for the moment. I know you're tired and the last 24 hours have been a nightmare." He stood then, Tess following. As they made their way toward the front door, Denny snapped his fingers.

"I almost forgot. Did Gary have any tattoos or piercings?" he asked, fully knowing about the partial phoenix on the man's chest.

"Yes. He had a phoenix. On his chest," Sarah said, making a confused face. "It was poorly done, and I was always telling him he should get it covered or changed. Why?"

"We just thought maybe it would help us understand him more. Do you know what it means?"

"Well, I'm not really sure. He didn't like talking about it much, said he got it when he was young and dumb. Those are his words, not mine," Sarah quickly added. "I think it looked almost like a home job—like a prison tattoo." she laughed nervously.

"Do you have a picture of it up close?" Denny asked carefully. Tess knew from the morning's meeting that the bottom half of the tattoo was missing, the inked flesh gone.

"Yes, of course," Sarah said, before leaving the couch and heading into the neighboring room. It looked to be a home office perhaps, although Tess couldn't be sure. Within moments, Sarah Hinsley came back into the room, and with a gently shaking hand, produced a snapshot of a smiling Gary Hinsley at the beach wearing nothing but a pair of green swim trunks. The Phoenix tattoo, in its entirety, was on full display.

Chapter Seven

Wednesday, October 26th, 11:43 a.m.

Across town in a small rundown apartment, a man sat at a rickety desk, typing into an old laptop. Although his surroundings weren't the greatest, they were a step up from his childhood—and for that the man was grateful. Anything was better than his childhood.

When he was young, as far back as he could remember, they had always been poor. His small family of two, consisting of his mother and himself, led a miserable existence. Every day was spent just trying to survive to the next. Not all the things from childhood had been bad, of course. He tried to think of the better times when his mind went to dark places. The good times were so few and far between though, that it was just a lot easier to dwell on the negative memories.

The man's life hadn't always been a shit storm. When he was first born, he and his mother had lived with his maternal grandparents in Columbus. For the first four or five years of his life, as he remembered it, he had a steady, loving home. His mom seemed happy in her own quiet way. He remembered her working two jobs when he was really young, coming home exhausted every day and having very little energy to play with him. It was during that time that his grandma died and then his grandfather shortly after, leaving his mom alone to raise a young son. His mom was barely an adult as it was, it seemed. So, alone in the world except for each other, the two moved into a small apartment not much better than the one he sat in now.

As he sat typing into his archaic laptop, he thought back to his shitty childhood once more. How there were often days when there would be nothing to eat in the house, how the electricity would get turned off regularly, or the landlord would come for rent that wasn't available.

At first, his mother had tried to make things work. She sold her parent's house, but after the lawyers and estate were settled, she got very little money. There was no other inheritance set aside for her or her son. She plastered a smile on her face though and pushed forward, trying to make a good life for her child.

After a couple of years of trying to succeed in Columbus, his mom decided to take a job in the small town of Crawley, in rural Ohio. "It'll be a new start for us, kiddo," she'd told him. He knew now that it wasn't a good new start. If anything, the move made their lives worse. The job hadn't panned out like she'd hoped, and her mental health began to decline. Raising a small boy alone, without enough income or family support, weighed heavily on his mother. Unbeknownst to him, the move to Crawley was the beginning of her end.

Despite her declining mental health and inability to provide a stable home for her son, she tried. He remembered going to the store the day before school would start each year, picking out an outfit they obviously couldn't afford. On the first day of school, his mom would dress him in the new outfit, taking care to hide the tags inside the clothes, and then drive him to the nicer end of town for pictures. She always took him to the same nice house on Maple St. It was a dark gray house with white trim and a big red door with a lion's head knocker in its center. His mom would make him hold up a chalkboard sign that read off his name, age, grade, and teacher's name while he stood quietly on the sidewalk in front of the house. She told him that it was a nice house and even though it wasn't their *real* house, nobody would know the difference.

She'd snap a few pictures for Facebook, then quickly usher him back to the car. Once in the vehicle, she'd have him strip out of the new clothes and into his older, thrift store rags. He never saw the new clothes again, and as he got older he realized she would return them to get the money back. Money she didn't have. He never knew if he should be mad at the fact that she was lying—lying about how good things were, with the new clothes and nice gray house in the background of all the school pictures. Mostly though, he just felt sad because of how pathetic the whole thing was.

When he was old enough to walk to the bus stop and get on the school bus alone, he started noticing a change in his mother. He was around eight years old or so at the time. It was little things at first: less food in the fridge, her coming home late at night. Then there were times when she started to not even come home at all. If he would ask her where she went every night, she'd get mad. He remembered the first time she struck him for asking. She'd been drinking and acting weird. He'd commented on it, his child mind trying to comprehend why she was acting that way. She'd gotten mad, turned around and smacked him across the face, her face angry and pinched. When he'd started to cry, surprised at the sudden outburst of violence, she'd begin to laugh at him. It was then, in that moment, that he knew something had definitely changed and that it wasn't good.

After the incident in the kitchen when his mother had slapped him, he kept to himself. It seemed that it was now up to him to cook his own food, if there was any. He'd also had to start bathing and dressing himself. It was hard at first to clean his clothes because they had no washing machine, and the laundromat was too far away to walk to. He just wore his three tee shirts over and over until even he couldn't stand his smell. He knew he smelled bad. The kids at school had made sure to tell him so almost daily, making sure to avoid sitting next to him on the bus or in the lunchroom. He heard the whispers and saw the stares. Even though he tried to ignore them, he'd often go home after school and cry himself to sleep while watching history documentaries on PBS.

When he discovered he could wash his clothes in the bathtub and then hang them around his room to dry, it was a whole new world—until the laundry soap ran out. During those few weeks when he felt clean and fresh, he'd almost felt happy, except for the gurgle of his empty belly. He'd bathe in the tub, taking care not to let the bar of soap soak in the water and disappear. After cleaning himself, he'd drain the old water, add some new, and wash his clothes when he'd dirtied them all. If his mother noticed, she never said anything.

She was never really around much then, except when she'd bring home random men late at night. He remembered lying on his mattress and listening to them talking loudly in the kitchen, slamming doors, and stumbling into the bedroom. Then he'd hear moans and grunts through the wall, something banging into the wall over and over. He would cover his head with his thrift store quilt, squeeze his eyes shut and try to fall asleep.

He was in middle school when he started wondering who his dad was. He'd asked previously when he was younger, but his mom always made excuses not to answer, always seeming to get upset. But one day when he asked her, as she sat at the rickety kitchen table, cigarette in one hand and picking at the chipped enamel tabletop with the other, she just stared into space. He was almost convinced that she wasn't going to answer him yet again when he noticed she was crying.

"Mom? Are you okay?" he'd asked, watching the tears stream down her face. He was starting to wish he'd never asked about his father again.

"No," came her whispered response. She sat in silence, staring straight ahead of her as though her mind was elsewhere. He sat across from her, taking in her frail frame and sunken cheeks. Even her hair had lost its luster.

"Your daddy is the devil," she finally said, picking at a scab on her arm. He'd noticed the red spots and scabs on her face and arms for a while now but never asked.

"The devil?" he'd asked, eyes round. "What do you mean?"

"The devil himself!" she yelled, suddenly slapping the table. He jumped, adrenaline coursing through him at her sudden outburst.

"Listen here, BJ," she said, not even bothering to use his given name, Brian, which irritated him. "I will tell you this one time, and one time only." She turned to look at him, her eyes lucid for once.

"I ain't gonna tell you his name... because I can't. I don't know," she said, looking down suddenly at the worn linoleum under the kitchen table. "There were too many to know for sure."

At fourteen, the boy's mind reeled. What was his mother saying? Was she a whore, like the kids at school had called her? He'd seen people whispering and staring at him and his mother when they'd go to the grocery, the laundromat, even the post office. Whispers had reached him on more than a handful of occasions. Mean whispers. Horrible whispers.

He remembered a time at school when Tawny Jacobs called his mom a druggie whore and said that she was asking to get raped, dressing and acting like that. He'd gotten so mad at Tawny, he'd attacked her. He'd sent her to the ER and got himself a free ride in the back of a police cruiser. Luckily for him, Tawny and her parents didn't press charges, and she was released from the hospital with only mild injuries. But that still didn't take away the sting of her words. Because, deep down, he thought that they might somehow be true.

Now, as he sat there at his computer, researching, he knew that he'd show those kids the truth—the name callers, the bullies, but most importantly, the devil himself.

Chapter Eight

Wednesday, October 26th, 12:30 p.m.

After leaving the Hinsleys' house and checking in with the school about Natalie once more, Tess and Denny were about to get something for lunch when Dr. Summers, the ME, called. Just as Denny had done with Natalie's call, he patched it through over the car's bluetooth as they traveled south toward Crawley.

"Haywood," he said, as a way of greeting.

"Detective Haywood, this is Abby Summers," came a disembodied female voice over the stereo. "I was just working on the autopsy of Mr. Hinsley, and well, there is something I think you should see. How soon could you be here?"

"We can be there by two," Denny said, glancing at the clock on the dashboard. "We are still a ways out. Just spoke with Hinsley's wife."

"Ummm 'we', sir?" Summers asked, sounding slightly confused.

"I have Deputy Dane with me. We've partnered up again, just like old times," he said with a grin at Tess.

"Oh! Hi, Tess!" Abby said cheerily. "I didn't realize you were listening. It's been a day, let me tell you! Just drive safe, guys. I'll see you soon." Before Denny or Tess could comment further, the ME ended the call.

"I wonder what she's found," said Tess aloud. She'd been quiet at the Hinsleys', unsure if she was meant to say or ask anything. Denny was the senior officer, and she wasn't keen to step on toes. She knew he'd never reprimand her in front of anyone, but she didn't want to do anything that would deserve one in the first place.

"Hopefully it's a break in the case," Denny said, pulling onto the interstate. "Basically, we have a guy that was friendly, unless he drank too much. Then he turned into a pushy asshole. But at least he was working on the drinking problem. The AA meetings at St. Catherine's. Maybe that's important; maybe it's not."

"Do you believe the wife? About them having the strongest marriage they've ever had?" Tess asked. "It seems like it's always the spouse or partner that does the killing. And it typically seems like it's over money or cheating."

"She seemed sincere enough, but that doesn't mean I'm just going to take her word for it. Until we find out more information, she's still on my list," Denny said, maneuvering his Tahoe around a slow-moving truck, laden down with bales of straw.

"I agree that she didn't seem like the type to do that stuff to her husband. Do you think she or any woman could tie a man in a boat, cover him with milk and honey to let the bugs eat him, and then lug another boat on top of him? It would take a super strong woman for all that lifting or more than one person. Whoever did it seems to be very motivated."

"Good point. Those boats weren't that small and lightweight. It took at least two people to flip the top one off of the bottom one when they were processing the crime scene," Denny said, pulling into a fast-food restaurant. They needed to grab lunch before heading to the medical examiner's office. The duo quickly ordered some burgers and fries, then hit the road again.

Tess was quiet for a few moments, chewing on some french fries and thinking. "Do you think that tattoo has anything to do with this?"

"What? Like he got killed because it looked bad, like a home job?" Denny said, giving her a grin. Tess rolled her eyes at him.

"No, silly. Like maybe it means something important?" Tess said, sticking another fry in her mouth. "I see people all the time with really bad tattoos. They don't get killed for them."

They rode in silence for a few moments, each lost in their own thoughts. Tess replayed the conversation with Mrs. Hinsley in her mind. The woman didn't appear to recognize Tess in any way, not even her name. Tess had kind of hoped Sarah would have given them a hint or reason as to why Tess's name was found at the crime scene. It still troubled her greatly to be associated with a crime scene, especially one so gruesome.

Wednesday, October 26th, 2:00 p.m.

Moments later, Denny pulled into the parking lot of a one storied brick building that housed the ME office. As Denny parked, Tess got a little nervous. She'd seen an autopsy once during police academy, but that corpse had been relatively fresh and not eaten away by insect activity and decomposition. What she was about to see would be much more involved. She'd seen the body of Gary Hinsley yesterday morning, but then he'd been crammed in a small boat and covered in maggots. Today, they would see exactly what wounds the poor man had endured.

Once the secretary had announced them, Denny and Tess were escorted to the autopsy bay where Dr. Abby Summers was clad in scrubs, gloves, and a face shield. Shoe covers and a cap completed the ensemble. She was writing something on a clipboard, while Stevie Nicks streamed out of the speakers on her computer. Abby looked up at them when they entered the suite, and a smile spread across her face.

"Hey guys!" She said, turning the music down. "You made good time. I was just finishing up some stuff."

The smell of the autopsy suite assaulted Tess's nose, but she chose to ignore it. The area was chilly and sterile. One wall of the room was made up of stainless-steel coolers for bodies. In the back of the room, another door led to what looked like another cooler room. The third wall consisted of shelves filled with boxes and jars of various specimens. Books filled part of the shelving near the computer where Dr. Summers stood. The floor, made up of pale gray tiles, looked clean. In the center of the room sat two gleaming stainless-steel tables with drains under each.

Tess looked away, suddenly heavy with the desire to flee. Death comes for us all, and no matter how much we may try to avoid it, there is always a curiosity that surrounds it.

It's part of what makes us human. Animals don't worry about such things. They live their lives, from day to day, never really worrying about death—if it will hurt, when it will happen. But humans know it's inevitable. Death, like paying taxes, comes to us all whether we like it or not.

Looking at the autopsy table, knowing she was about to witness something hideous and horrible, made Tess's stomach begin to churn. A primal urge to separate herself from the current situation came over her.

"What do you say, Tess?" Denny's voice caught her attention, tearing it away from the dark thoughts swarming in her head.

"I'm sorry. What did you say?" She asked, pulling her gaze away from the table.

"Shall we get started?" Denny said, giving her a strange look. "Dr. Summers asked us to wear these." He tossed a pair of blue shoe covers to Tess. He nodded to some gowns hanging on a hook behind them. "Suit up."

As Tess slipped the booties over her shoes and donned the gown, she watched as Dr. Summers opened one of the steel coolers lining the far wall. With little effort the doctor pulled out a rack with a body bag holding the earthly remains of Gary Hinsley.

"So, after finishing the autopsy of Mr. Hinsley, I would say the manner of death is definitely homicide. Cause of death is…exposure, blood loss, dehydration, insect activity perimortem. Take your pick," Dr. Summers said, wheeling the body over to the table in the center of the room. She unzipped the body bag and the smell of decomposition instantly increased exponentially. Tess and Denny each stepped back out of reflex and then leaned in to see the remains.

The body of Gary Hinlsey lay bare before them. Or, rather, what was left of him. He'd been rinsed and cleansed since the last time Tess had seen him, but she was still not ready for what she was seeing. Her eyes started at his head, taking in his mottled skin and the darkened holes where his eyes once were. What remained of his lips were gnarled back, revealing the white bone of his teeth, his face forever in a grimace. All along his torso, red, open sores peppered his skin, evidence of the insects that had feasted on him. The crude "Y" incision on his chest extended down to what was left of his abdomen. Tess remembered from the crime scene that his abdomen had taken most of the trauma from the insects.

Her eyes drifted lower, and she let out a slight gasp, looking up at Denny and then Abby.

"Was he… emasculated?" She asked in horror. Denny's face soured, and he shifted his legs together. Dr. Summers nodded.

"I'm afraid so," she said as she opened the body bag further so that they could see the lower half of the body better. "At first, there was too much going on. Blood, fluids... maggots... pieces of flesh. But once I washed him and did his external exam, it was obvious. His entire genitalia is gone and somebody did it to him antemortem."

"You mean he was alive when they did that?" Denny said, his face going pale.

"Unfortunately, yes," Dr. Summers said, pointing to the stub of the body's manhood. "It looks like a crude dissection, probably from a serrated knife or a dulled hunting knife. Not sharp like a filet knife or scalpel blade. This was meant to hurt, to inflict the most pain possible. The amount of clotted blood around the remaining part of the genitalia and found at the crime scene—I looked at the crime scene photos to confirm—was quite substantial."

"Enough to kill him?" Tess asked, studying the corpse in front of her.

"Not at first, no. Usually, if male genitalia is cut off, say by freak accident or foul play, it would eventually clot but would need medical attention straight away. In the case of this man, he was probably emasculated and then dumped in the boat to die slowly. Eventually, if bleeding didn't get him, infection would have. With Mr. Hinsley here, he was also force-fed milk and honey, just like you suggested, Tess," the doctor said, reaching for a jar on the counter behind her. She held it up, the contents sloshing.

"Stomach contents," she said simply. "There was no actual food in his stomach or small intestines, indicating that he hadn't eaten anything for a couple of days prior to death, except the honey mixture."

"How can you tell he was force-fed the honey and didn't just drink it on command?" Denny asked, avoiding looking directly at the jar in the doctor's hand.

"Bruising. I found it in the back of his throat and along his esophagus. Most likely made by a rubber hose of some kind being forced down his throat into his stomach. I found remnants of honey in the throat and oral cavity." She paused for a second and then pointed toward the tattoo. "As for this tat, I'd say you're looking at a home job for sure."

"How can you tell?" Tess asked.

"Well, for one, it's not very good," Summers said, with a grin. "But seriously, though, the ink itself isn't very pigmented. Typically, amateur ink isn't as nice and it's more superficial, meaning they don't age well." She set the jar of stomach contents down and then pointed toward the bottom of the tattoo, where the lower half of the phoenix was missing. "We can't see what the Phoenix held in his claws because of the insect activity postmortem."

"Don't worry, we have a photo," said Denny, pulling out the photograph that Sarah Hinsley had given them. Dr. Summers leaned over and looked at it, unimpressed. She shrugged.

"Nothing exciting. Just... What is that? Some kind of flower?" She shrugged again, pointing to the bottom of the tattoo in the picture. "Look, I don't know what this tattoo means, if anything. All I know is that this guy was emasculated prior to death, then starved and dehydrated for a few days, except for the milk and honey, and then died. Death would have happened from blood loss, exposure, and from the insects entering every orifice they could find and eating him from the inside out. The milk and honey would have attracted some of the insects. The scent of blood would have attracted others."

Chapter Nine

Wednesday, October 26th, 3:32 p.m.

After leaving the ME's office, Denny and Tess headed over to pick Natalie up from school. They also stopped to let out Otter before the evening debriefing. While Natalie sat and did her homework at Tess's kitchen table, Tess put some homemade chocolate chip cookies in the oven to bake. Once Natalie and Otter were content, Tess slipped into the living room and sat down next to Denny who was reading something on his phone.

"Everything okay?" she asked, handing him a glass of sweet tea. He looked up and grinned when he saw the tea.

"My favorite. You remembered."

"Of course I remembered. We were partners for two years," Tess said, giving him an amused look. "Probably still would be partners if you hadn't gone all BCI on me."

Denny laughed, the sound making Tess smile. "You knew I was always wanting to be a detective, even when I was hauling your rookie ass around." He took a long swig of the tea. "Why don't you take the detective exam? You seem to have a good eye for it. You don't want to stay on patrol forever, like Ricky Osbourne, do you?"

Tess knew he'd added that last jab about Ricky just to annoy her. She turned to him and rolled her eyes. "Seriously? No way. I'd rather stab my own hand with a knife than hang out with Osbourne for any length of time." She made a gagging face and then giggled.

"Is he still pestering you for a date?" Denny asked, wiggling his eyebrows at her. She rewarded him with another eye roll.

"I've turned him down every time but he keeps at it," Tess said, folding her arms across her chest and leaning her head back on the couch to rest. "Persistent. Doesn't take no for an answer."

"Maybe you're too nice about it?" Denny asked, taking another sip of his tea.

Tess sighed. Denny knew her too well. "I always tell him 'no thanks, not tonight,' or 'sorry, I already have plans'. You'd think he'd figure it out by now."

"Why don't you just tell him to go fuck himself?" Denny asked, raising an eyebrow at her from over his glass. Tess felt her face turn red and cringed inwardly.

"Because for one, I may be a cop, but I'm a lady. I don't want to be rude. And secondly, I don't use language like that, and you know it!" Tess said, throwing a pillow from the couch at him. Denny just busted out laughing at her reaction, knowing that she was getting flustered. Just then, the kitchen timer went off, and Tess got up to get the cookies out of the oven to cool. She sensed Denny following her into the kitchen and smiled to herself. While he quietly talked to Natalie at the kitchen table, Tess pulled the sheet of cookies from the oven and set them on the stove.

Suddenly, Denny was right next to her, hovering over the cookies with hungry eyes. When he reached for one, Tess smacked his hand away.

"Hey! Watch it! You'll burn yourself!" she scolded, but it didn't seem to stop him. He grabbed one, and then with a smile on his face, shifted it from one hand to the other.

"Hot?" Tess asked, giving him a look. She pulled down a plate from the cabinet, slid two cookies onto it and took it over to the table for Natalie. Looking at the girl, she said, "Don't be stubborn like your dad. Let them cool."

Natalie grinned and nodded. She and Tess turned then and watched as Denny tried to take a bite of the hot cookie and then open mouth panted before swallowing the molten treat. Tess just shook her head, and Natalie rolled her eyes.

Wednesday, October 26th, 6:00 p.m.

Right on time that night, the investigative group reconvened at the sheriff's department. Sheriff Burrows sat in the same seat he'd sat in that morning watching as everyone began to trickle in. Denny and Tess sat down and quietly waited for the daily debriefing to start. It had been a long day. Tess would rather be back at her house with Denny and Natalie like this afternoon, but instead Natalie had to go stay at Denny's neighbor's house while they attended the meeting.

Tess was mildly surprised that she'd even had the thought, but she'd be lying to herself if she said she wasn't happy to be working side by side with Denny again. She'd had a schoolgirl crush on him while she was at the academy, as did some of the other cadets. As she'd started working with him on the job as a rookie, her crush had grown into feelings of friendship and respect. He was married then and also her superior, not that that changed anything really. Even if he'd been single, as he was now, there was no way she'd push for something more. She was sure he harbored no romantic feelings toward her, and she would rather keep his friendship than mess things up with him.

"Okay, people," Sheriff Burrows said, jarring Tess's mind back to reality. "I know it's dinner time and everyone is tired, but let's see what progress we've made in this case. Umm... Seawell, what do you have for us?"

The crime scene tech cleared his throat and opened his file. "Well sir, I worked on identifying the make and model of shoe that made the impression near the shoreline of Lake Amelia. It appears to have been made by a pair of hiking boots, more specifically, Keens. Although it's a partial print, there is enough of it to show that the shoe was a men's size 8 or women's 10. Given the width of it, I'm assuming it's a men's shoe. There was enough of a wear pattern on them that it would be helpful if we could compare it to a suspect's shoe," Mike Seawell said, looking around the table as everyone listened.

"There are different characteristics of footwear. Like, for instance, different wear patterns. Not everyone steps down or carries themselves in the same exact way as the next person." He pointed to Claybourne. "You might walk with your feet rolled more inward than Denny, and that would make your shoes wear out in a different area of the sole than Denny's. Or say you stepped on a nail, and it tore up part of the rubber on your tread. That imperfection would leave a telling mark when found at a scene and could be compared to a suspect's shoe. It's what we call an individual characteristic."

"Good work, Mike," Burrows said, shuffling through some papers in front of him. "Any news on the red fiber found at the scene?"

"Under microscopic examination, it appears to be dyed wool, most likely from something like a hat, sweater, mittens, that sort of thing."

"How can you tell it's wool and not another type of animal fiber?" Detective Malone asked curiously.

"Well, animal fibers are made up of four things: keratin, hydrogen, nitrogen, and some carbon. What makes wool special is that it is the only natural animal fiber that contains a bit of sulfur as well."

"Ok, so we are looking for a homicidal, red wool wearing, hiker donning a pair of worn-out boots? Got it," Claybourne said dismally. "That could be anybody."

"Denny, Tess, how did things go with the wife?" Burrows asked, ignoring Claybourne's attempt at self-pity.

"Well, considering," Denny said. He turned and looked at Tess. "You want to tell them what we learned?"

"Sure," Tess said, opening the notes app on her phone. Looking up at Sheriff Burrows, she began. "Mrs. Hinsley was obviously mourning but was able to discuss her husband with us. Apparently he was the life of the party but would turn into a mean drunk. He had a problem with alcohol but was in AA meetings at St. Catherines every Thursday evening. He'd been sober for quite a while now. As for the tattoo, Dr. Summers confirmed that it was poorly done, most likely an amateur." She pulled out the photograph of Gary Hinsley at the beach. "Here is a photo of the deceased with the complete tattoo on full display." She handed it to the sheriff who glanced at it and passed it around the table. "There appears to be some kind of flowers in the phoenix's claws. I have yet to identify the type, sir, but will research them tonight."

"They look like the flowers my wife has in our backyard," Claybourne commented. "I forget what exactly they are though. Let me text her." He began typing into his phone. Almost instantly, his phone beeped with an incoming text. "She says they are hyacinths." His phone buzzed again, and he read the texts, "She said that blue and purple hyacinths signify regret and sincerity—and that if I'm late for dinner again tonight I better bring her some to apologize."

Hoots and laughter filled the room as Claybourne hung his head and made an exaggerated face. Sheriff Burrows cleared his throat after a moment. "OK people, let's get back on track. And Claybourne... don't forget the flowers for your wife." A rare grin covered his face.

"Maybe the tattoo is important after all," Tess said, a thought coming to her. "Think about it. If the hyacinth means regret or 'I'm sorry' and the phoenix symbolizes rising above something or rebirth, then maybe the whole thing together means that Gary was sorry for something but was trying to move on?"

Silence filled the room for a moment as everyone thought about what Tess had said. She nervously sat there for a second and then wrote down her thoughts in her notes.

"Not bad, Deputy Dane," the sheriff said, with an appreciative nod. "That makes sense. Until we know the true meaning, let's try to prove or disprove that theory for the tattoo. Did the wife say anything about it?"

"No, sir," Denny said, "All she could tell us was that he never wanted to talk about it—and that she didn't like it much."

"Well, it is rather... different," someone mumbled under their breath, though Tess couldn't tell who.

"Did Dr. Summers tell you anything when you were there today?" the sheriff inquired, taking a sip of water from his cup on the table in front of him.

Denny nodded, "Yeah, the poor guy was... emasculated." A collective sucking in of air sounded throughout the room.

"Like somebody took his nuts...and everything?" Malone said, looking ill. Denny nodded.

"Doc said it looked like it happened prior to death. Extremely painful because the possible knife used was either dull or jagged due to the rough edges of the wound." Tess said. "Mr. Hinsley's abdomen was indeed filled with evidence of milk and honey, just as we guessed this morning. There was bruising in his throat and esophagus, most likely from being force-fed. He was tortured to death."

Just then, there was a knock at the door, and Ricky Osbourne stuck his head in. Sheriff Burrows looked up at him, a scowl on his face from being interrupted.

"What is it, Osbourne?" he barked.

"I'm sorry, sir, but there's another body."

Chapter Ten

Brian sat on a broken-down couch in his living room, the rough, musty material rubbing at his bare skin. He sat shirtless, wearing nothing but a pair of gym shorts and a smug look. He grinned at the TV as the news anchor announced a "grisly discovery" after a body was found "tortured to death" out at Lake Amelia. *Good. Somebody found ol' Gary,* Brian thought to himself. *The son of a bitch deserved so much more than he got.* But Brian didn't have the time or energy to spend on just one of the people on his list. His work wasn't done yet. And the best was yet to come.

He'd always remember the day he learned the truth. The truth of his beginning, and his mother's end. From all accounts, his mother had been a happy kid and came from a close-knit family. She'd been an honors student in highschool and had excelled in English and writing. But something happened one night, long ago, during her senior year. She'd changed that night, turned into a different version of herself and had shut down. She'd spend days locking herself into her room, barely eating.

Brian was born nine months later.

He knew all of this because he'd found her diary, hidden away among her things, after she'd passed away. The things he'd read inside had scalded his soul. No wonder his mother had become a shell of her former self, turning to drugs and alcohol to soothe the monsters in her mind. In that moment, when he'd read the truth, his mother became so clear, so...agonizingly human...to him that he'd fallen to his knees and sobbed. It was almost as though he could feel her trauma, her pain—physical and emotional. The diary explained so much about her, about him, and about their pathetic existence.

But he wasn't about to dwell in self-pity over the past, over things he had no control of. Times had changed, and for the first time, the power was in *his* hands. He had vowed that day, while reading the diary, that he would make the guilty parties pay, one way or another.

The cops had already found Gary. Poor miserable Gary, crying and pleading for his life. Pathetic. Brian had no sympathy for the disgusting piece of human garbage that was Gary Hinsley. That sack of shit acted like he didn't even know what Brian was talking about at first. And yet, despite all the crying and snot, when Brian started reading aloud the contents of the diary, Gary's eyes had become large, the screaming more intense. And then, when the contents of Gary's bladder had emptied down his own leg, Brian took a knife and cut off the most offending piece of him.

Now, as Brian sat there reliving the moment he'd shoved Gary into the boats, bleeding and lying in his own piss, he felt amazing—euphoric, even. His plan was coming together perfectly after months of researching and planning.

His ears perked up as the sound of multiple sirens came blaring down the street and past his apartment. *Sounds like they found the second man on my list*, he mused. With that thought, he let out a laugh, wishing he could see their faces.

Chapter Eleven

Wednesday, October 26th, 7:32 p.m.

Tess gripped the dashboard as Denny took a right onto Camden Mill Rd. It was almost dark and the flashing blue and red lights on the roof of the Tahoe cast an eerie glow on the passing trees. The rural road, shouldered by old-growth trees on either side, held a few houses. Toward the end of the road, their destination sat: the Old Camden Mill. Since it closed down some thirty years ago, the mill building itself, complete with an old water wheel and outbuildings, had sat empty. No one except teenagers looking to party or hookup came out this far nowadays. Tess hadn't been there since sophomore year when Joey Pike had invited her out to a weekend party. It had been her first, and last, time getting drunk. Just thinking about the hangover she'd had then made her grip the dashboard harder.

"You know, you can slow down," she said, her stomach lurching as Denny took another curve in the road. "Won't do any good if we die on the way to a crime scene."

"Noted," Denny said, slowing the vehicle a minuscule amount. As they rounded the bend, the old mill came into view, shrouded in shadows. Flashing lights of the first responders' vehicle blinded them as they pulled over on the shoulder of the road. Right behind them, Mike Seawell and his forensic team pulled to a stop.

"What do we have?" Denny asked as he got out of the vehicle and approached the waiting officer.

"Deceased male. Kids called it in," the male officer said. "They are over there." He pointed to a trio of teenagers huddled together, some crying. "They say they were out here to study plants for a botany class, which I don't believe for a second. It's dark, and they smell like weed."

"Can you show us the body?" Denny asked, glancing around the dark surroundings. The sun had officially set, and the entire woods and mill were nearly pitch black except for the flashing lights of the cruiser and a few flashlights.

"Sure. Officer Bailey is back there now, on guard. I was about to question the kids. You know, divide and conquer," the officer said. Tess glanced at his name tag: T. Wiggins, Crawley PD. Tess had never met him but then again, she worked for the Swain County Sheriff's Office. Since the mill was closer to Crawley than Camden Town, the county seat, it made sense that they'd respond first.

"Just follow that path over there," Wiggins said, pointing to a trail of trampled overgrown grass that was barely wider than an animal tract. "That'll take you to the mill. Officer Bailey's waiting on you. And ma'am, you might want to rethink about going back there," he said, looking at Tess. "It's pretty awful."

"So is your patronizing tone, sir," Tess bristled, shocking herself. "Believe me. I've seen some pretty messed up stuff in the past thirty six hours." And with that, she turned on her heel and headed toward the trail.

"Wow, what was that about?" Denny whispered when he came up behind her. "That was very unlike you. I *kinda* like Spicy Tess." He wiggled his eyebrows at her jokingly. She snorted.

"Shut it, Haywood, or you can sit in the Tahoe and wait for me," Tess said, grinning at him across the flashlights beam. "I didn't like his tone. And I don't know, I wasn't in the mood to deal with it."

They walked in silence for a few moments, the dewy grass slapping at their legs as they passed by. The chill of the late October night crept into Tess's jacket, and she shivered involuntarily.

"So, why did we get called to this scene if Crawley was the first responder?" Tess asked. "Is it just a normal dead body or another scene that will haunt my dreams for the rest of my days?"

"I don't know for sure yet, but I'm guessing it's pretty bad or they wouldn't have called us. Crawley only has what... three officers?" Denny said as they approached a light up ahead. It appeared that Officer Bailey had positioned a dual halogen tripod light at the old mill to illuminate the scene.

As Tess and Denny entered the immediate lighted area surrounding the mill house, Tess gasped. The sight in front of her was both shocking and grotesque.

Before her was the old mill and there, hanging from the water wheel, were the remains of a man, broken and bloodied.

His limbs, crushed and bent at odd angles, were pulled away from his body as though he was crucified there. What remained of his head appeared beaten in, his face a pulpy mess. Blood, now dried and clotted, stained his naked skin. Tess noticed that the man's genitals were missing and all that remained was a bloody mess. She gulped at the thought that he, too, had been emasculated.

"Dear God in Heaven..." mumbled Denny as he shined his flashlight around the scene. The beam of light cast otherworldly shadows over the area making it even more eerie.

"Detective," the waiting policeman said, stepping forward. "I'm Officer Bailey, Crawley PD." The man shook Denny's hand and then Tess's. "Ma'am," he said with a nod.

"Detective Haywood, BCI. This is my partner, Deputy Dane with the Swain County Sheriff's office," Denny said, indicating Tess.

"Nice to meet you," Tess said politely. "What do we know so far?"

"Not much really. It's too dark and overgrown around here to get over there easily," Bailey said, pointing toward the body on the water wheel. "I tried to go around that way, by the edge of the water, but it was all muddy. I saw some footprints and drag marks near the grass and decided to just stand still and look with my flashlight instead of getting too close. I figure we'll have to wait until sunup to get a full picture of what the hell happened here." He pulled out his phone. "I did snap some pictures of the shoe prints and drag marks, but I don't know if they will be of any help."

"Did you take any photos of the body before the sun went down?" Denny asked, watching the young officer.

"Well... yeah, I took a couple—for evidence," Bailey quickly added.

"I know you wouldn't use those photos for personal use so if you don't mind emailing or texting them to me before you delete them, that would be great," Denny said before looking away, back at the body. Bailey looked slightly guilty and glanced down at his feet for a second.

"Any ID or personal effects?" Tess asked. Bailey shook his head.

"We've only gotten this close to him, and I haven't found anything obvious in the grass or water." Bailey offered, guiding them closer to the water wheel.

As they got closer, the breeze shifted, bringing with it the sour rotten stench of death. Tess schooled her expression, unwilling to show weakness at this scene, even though inwardly bile churned in her stomach.

Denny made a pass with his flashlight, the beam illuminating the waterlogged footprints in the mud near the water's edge. Casting the light toward the body, Denny made a face when the trio saw that the man's chest and face seemed to be moving in undulating waves.

"God...as if this isn't bad enough, there has to be maggots too?" Bailey said, turning away and walking back to the trail.

"Is it bad that I don't really mind the maggots?" Tess whispered to Denny as they skirted around the mud. "The smell seems more offensive to me."

Denny snickered, "You really are something, you know that? First you get spicy with Officer Tough Guy and now you're admitting that you like maggots? I can't wait to see what tomorrow brings."

By this point, the two found themselves on the opposite side of the water wheel, back behind it where the weeds were long and gnarled. More worried about ticks than maggots, Tess moved closer to the scene, casting her light to and fro in front of her.

"We need to get him off of there. Can't they bring more lights?" she asked. Denny nodded toward the crime scene crew, led by Mike Seawell, as they approached the scene opposite them. They watched as the group took in the scene and heard murmurs as Seawell and Bailey discussed something, Bailey gesticulating wildly.

Seawell and his two crime scene technicians began setting up more lights and organizing their equipment, while Bailey began setting up crime scene tape to cordon off the area. Though that should have been done in the first place, the darkness had made it difficult to determine where the crime scene ended and the forest began.

The group, Denny and Tess included, began working the scene. The flash of the camera illuminated the dark sky like lightning at times, the murmurs of the crime techs filling the air.

After a while, Tess heard another car pull up to the road through the trees and moments later, Dr. Abby Summers came into view. Making her way over the uneven ground, flashlight in hand, Abby slowly stumbled over to Denny and Tess.

The three of them stood silent for a moment as Summers took in the scene for herself. Shaking her head in dismay, she shined her light up and down the dead man's body multiple times before turning to Denny.

"What is wrong with people?" She asked incredulously. She sighed, "Do we know anything about him? Any ID?"

"Not yet," Denny said. "They haven't found any clothes or items that would identify the man. His face is a bloody pulp so that's not going to help much. There's so much blood on his body it's almost too hard to determine race. The lividity in his legs doesn't help either." Denny pointed to the mottled, purple flesh caused by pooling of blood and fluids under the skin.

"Well, let's get him down from there, get him to my lab, and see what he tells us," Abby said. "After all, they say dead men tell no tales, unless you're in forensics."

Chapter Twelve

Thursday, October 27th, 12:42 a.m.

It was well after midnight when Denny dropped Tess off at her house. They were both exhausted. The processing of the crime scene had stretched into the late, cool hours of the night. Tess just wanted a shower and to be snuggled up with Otter in bed.

The Labrador greeted her at the front door, toy in his mouth as normal. He wiggled in a full body wag and made a throaty whine of excitement.

"Hey boy," Tess said, bending to rub the dog's black head. "Sorry it was such a long day, bud. I'm glad we got that doggie door, huh?" She stood back up and smiled down at Otter. As she walked into the kitchen and flipped on the light, Otter followed her, his nails softly clicking on the wood floor.

"Want a snack?" she asked the dog as she washed her hands. "I haven't eaten since that cookie this afternoon, and I'm starved." She tossed a couple of treats in the air, watching with a grin as the dog caught every last one, then set about making herself a small meal.

Carrying it to the table, she sat down and opened her laptop. Munching on her turkey sandwich, she began researching what she had seen that night—the wheel; the broken body of a man hanging from it. Did it all mean something? Was it somehow connected to Gary Hinsley's killing? She was too amped up from the scene, from the whole day actually, and knew she wouldn't be able to fall asleep easily. Knowing that she needed to be her best tomorrow, and ready to go at the sheriff's 8 o'clock meeting, didn't deter her.

It only took a few moments before she found it. A website popped up talking about the Breaking Wheel, a medieval way to torture criminals prior to death. According to the online post, the victim would be broken by repeatedly dropping a heavy wooden wheel with a metal spike or rim sticking out of it onto the victim. Starting at the person's legs and then moving upwards to the arms, the bones were snapped one by one as the victim howled in agony. Once the body was a limp, broken version of itself, it would be woven between the spokes of the wheel or hung up and tied to the wheel. If all of that didn't kill the prisoner, then they would be decapitated, burned alive, or left for the birds to eat their flesh.

Tess slammed her laptop closed, suddenly feeling the sandwich she'd just eaten threatening to come back up. Her mind going a million miles a minute, she grabbed her phone and texted Denny, *check this out*, as she sent the link to him.

She quickly ran to the bathroom, stripped her clothes, and slid beneath the hot water of the shower head. She needed to scrub her hair, her body, to remove all the horribleness she'd been a part of that day. She'd scrub her mind if she could.

Who was killing men by using old torture methods? And why? Her mind continued to race as she stepped out of the shower, wrapping a plush white towel around herself. Hearing her phone buzz with an alert, she went to the living room where she'd left it.

Three texts and a missed call from Denny, each one more urgent than the last. She tapped his number, and he answered on the first ring.

"How can you send me that link and then not answer your phone?" He asked excitedly but not unkindly. "That Breaking Wheel is horrible. How do you find this stuff?

"Just research. It's called Google," Tess teased, a smile crossing her face, despite the dark subject hanging over their heads.

"Yeah, yeah," Denny said, his voice sounding tired. "You think we have some psycho serial killer out there, taking men out by emasculation and torture?"

She knew he was trying to make a joke of the obvious, in an attempt to relieve some of the dread surrounding them.

"Unfortunately, yes," she said with a sigh, as she tightened the towel around herself before sitting on the couch next to Otter. "I don't know why or how, but I think these two killings are connected. It's pretty messed up," she sighed. "On the bright side, at least my name wasn't scrawled anywhere this time."

"Oh, Tess," Denny said sympathetically. "I don't know why your name was at that scene yesterday, but we will find out. If this is too much for you, just say the word. And no, before you get all defensive, I'm not downplaying you because you're a woman. You've been through a lot, with the academy, down at the station." He paused for a moment. "How is your dad doing? I haven't asked in a while—and for that, I'm sorry."

"Oh, the usual I guess," Tess said with a sigh. "Sometimes he recognizes me, sometimes he doesn't. I still go to visit a couple of times a week regardless of if he's lucid or not."

"I'm sorry, Tess," Denny replied, concern in his deep voice. "He's still so young. He shouldn't be struggling with dementia at this age. He should still be working cases, throwing the bad guys in the slammer. He was a great cop."

"Thanks, Denny," Tess said, willing herself not to get too emotional. "That really means a lot. And yes, he is too young for all this mess. He's barely sixty."

"You still carry his old service revolver and tape recorder?" he asked, a smile in his voice.

"You know I do. Always have, always will," Tess replied, leaning back into the couch and petting Otter. The dog let out a contented sigh at the affection.

"How's your mom?" Denny asked carefully. Tess rolled her eyes, just thinking about her mother.

"Oh, you know, living the life down in Florida with her man of the month," Tess replied, contempt in her voice. "I don't speak to her, and it's not from my lack of trying. When she left dad, she left me as well. Who does that? They were married for nearly twenty five years, but the minute he got his diagnosis, she couldn't be bothered."

"Some people are too selfish for their own good, Tess. And it isn't you or your dad's fault."

"I know," Tess sighed, wiping at a tear that was threatening to escape her eye. "I just had to take care of Dad all by myself during those early years of his disease. All while finishing high school and then attending the academy. I was what...sixteen when she left?" She sighed again. "I don't mean to whine about it all, but I really could have used her help. I tried to stay in contact for a while, but she began avoiding my calls, so I eventually gave up. I get my updates about her from my Aunt Rosie."

"Well, you seem to have done a great job," Denny complimented. "You finished school and academy, got your father the help he needed when his disease progressed, and now you have a good job. Your partner isn't so bad either," he added, lightening the mood.

Tess laughed, "True. You're pretty awesome. I mean if you can get past all the moodiness."

"Moodiness?" Denny asked with a quiet laugh. "I'm not moody."

"Whatever. You keep telling yourself that. I've seen you before your coffee kicks in and brings you back to life. I've seen you getting frustrated when interrogating people you know are guilty. Shoot, I've even seen you sulking about after the sheriff's gotten on you about something. You're moody," Tess said, a smile in her voice.

Denny laughed again, "I guess you have a point. See you tomorrow, Tess. Pick you up around 7:30?"

"Sounds good. See you then." Tess said before hanging up her phone. She headed to bed, Otter following close behind.

Chapter Thirteen

Thursday, October 27th, 11:24 a.m.

Denny and Tess made their way across the street to Cody Kneaper's house, a few doors down from Gary Hinsley's address. Sarah Hinsley had mentioned that the two men had bonded over the grill, and Denny wanted to ask him a few questions.

Hoping to glean some new information, Denny walked up to the front door of the light blue ranch style house and rang the doorbell. There was no answer at first, despite the car parked in the driveway. Denny rang the bell again as Tess patiently waited.

"Can I help you?" asked a middle-aged man coming around the side of the house, a pair of headphones dangling around his thick neck.

"Hi, are you Cody Kneaper?" Denny inquired with a friendly smile.

"Sure am," the man said. "You're here about Gary, aren't you?"

Tess and Denny nodded. Cody smiled grimly and beckoned them to follow him around the house. They follow him down a brick path leading to the back yard. There, scattered across the patio, were parts of a dismantled lawn mower.

"Damn thing quit working on me," Cody explained motioning toward the scattered parts. "Thought I'd get one more mow in for the season but it's not looking so good." He paused for a moment, moving some tools out of the way and gesturing for the officers to have a seat. Waiting until they were seated on his turquoise lawn furniture, he then took a seat himself.

"So, have you found out anything about what happened to Gary?" Cody asked, watching Tess and Denny closely.

"Well, that is what we are hoping you can help us with, Mr. Kneaper," Tess said, taking the lead. "As I'm sure you know by now, we've talked to his wife, Sarah. She mentioned that you and her husband were pretty close. Would you agree with that statement?"

"Sure," Cody said, scratching his large stomach for a second. "We would talk about cars and stuff. Grill out a few times a month during the summers. They'd bring their kids down to play with ours. My kids are a year or so older than the twins. And Sarah seemed to like Lucy, my wife. It was an instant friendship. You know... when you just seem to click with someone?"

"Yeah, I get that," Tess said with a warm smile and a nod. "How long have you guys been neighbors?"

Cody scrunched his face up, thinking for a moment. "I'd have to guess about...four years or so? Their twins were still small at the time. I remember when they took their Little Tikes toy cars out, and our kids got so excited. Before we knew it, all the kids were doing laps while Gary and I stood there chatting." He smiled at the memory.

"Sounds like a fun time," Tess agreed with a smile. She paused for a moment, then pressed on. "Did you and Gary ever talk about the state of their marriage? Did you ever sense any tension?"

"No. Gary didn't really have anything negative to say about Sarah—or anybody really. He was a nice guy, maybe got a little pushy and loud when he got drunk, but nothing extreme. And no, I never heard them fighting. They always seemed to get along."

"Do you know if he had any enemies? Angry customers at the garage?"

"Not that I know of. He didn't really talk about work much, just said it was tiring and stressful at times," Cody said, with a sigh. "I'm sorry. I'm not being very helpful, am I?"

"You're doing fine," Tess said, smiling warmly. "Have you seen anybody hanging around their house? Someone that doesn't quite belong?"

Cody was quiet for a moment, a look of concentration etching into his face. Finally, he said, "I know pretty much everyone on this street. Nobody new around here recently that I remember." He sighed again, looking at his feet.

Suddenly, he looked up excitedly, "Wait! You know what....? Now that I think about it, there was somebody. It was a couple of weeks ago though."

"Go on," Tess encouraged. Cody nodded and then stood up and began to pace.

"Yes. I remember it now. It was....." he paused to think again. "It was a Monday if I remember right. I'd gotten home late from football practice with the kids and didn't think much about it at the time. The kids were hungry, and I was tired. We drove by him, and I remember I waved. He was sitting in his car and ignored me. He was too busy looking at a house—the Hinsleys' house."

"Do you remember what kind of car he drove? Or maybe even what he looked like?"

"White guy, younger," Cody said. "He was maybe mid to late twenties? He was wearing a beanie cap and *kinda* sat hunched in his seat, peaking out. I thought it was a little weird. As for the car, it was dark. Black maybe. Older model. Might have been a Toyota or a Honda. I don't really remember. As I said, I was dealing with wrangling the kids and didn't pay much attention."

"Awesome," Tess said with a smile. "You've been helpful. I think that is all the questions we have currently. We'll stay in touch." Taking out a business card, she handed it to the man. "If you think of anything else, or if you see the man again, please call us."

"Certainly. Will do," Cody said, taking Tess's proffered hand and giving it a gentle but firm shake.

They said their goodbyes then left and headed back to the station. Once they were in the car, Tess sighed while looking out the window.

"What's wrong?" Denny asked, putting on his sunglasses even though it wasn't overly bright out.

"I don't know. I keep thinking about that poor guy last night and wondering how all this is connected," she pondered. "How I'm connected to it all."

"I'm hoping we can ID the guy on the Breaking Wheel soon. I got a text from Mike at the crime lab while we were talking to Cody Kneaper. He said that a partial print they found on the wheel wasn't enough to get a positive match on AFIS. The print was smudged and only had a few good ridges. So, either our perp isn't in the system, or we'll have to get a better print next time," Denny sighed.

"God, I hope there isn't a next time," Tess said, buckling her seat belt as Denny pulled the Tahoe away from the curb. "These two murders are enough!"

Chapter Fourteen

Thursday, October 27th, 2:15 p.m.

While Denny was at Natalie's school meeting with the principal about the bullying his daughter was enduring, Tess decided to spend some time with Otter. She'd been spending so much time working on the case at the station and at home each night that Tess felt Otter had been neglected.

Clipping on his leash, she decided to walk him down the street to the local dog park for some play time. After locking her front door and pocketing her keys, she and the dog made their way down the leaf-strewn sidewalk. Otter excitedly walked beside her, tail wagging while Tess led him, deep in thought.

Cody Kneaper had seen a man in his mid to late twenties watching the Hinsley residence. The timing seemed right for someone to be casing the house, but why would someone stalk Gary Hinsley? So far, Tess and Denny had only been able to dig up that Gary was a rough drunk. Even Malone had told Denny that Gary's coworkers had nothing bad to say about him. For all intents and purposes, Gary Hinsley was squeaky clean. Or was he?

And what about the John Doe at the Old Camden Mill? How did he play into all of this? Were the killings at random or somehow connected? Tess sighed, her brain going a mile a minute with various possibilities, but none of them seemed to fit.

As Tess approached the dog park, she noticed her neighbor, Tim, and his Bernese Mountain Dog, Nora, playing ball. Otter saw them too and began whining and full body wagging. Nora dropped her ball and came running toward Tess and Otter as they came inside the fence. Unclipping the leash, she laughed as Nora and Otter took off playing and chasing each other. Waving at Tim from across the field, Tess meandered around the perimeter, watching the dogs enjoy the social time.

The sun had decided to come out from behind the clouds for once, and Tess enjoyed the cool air mixed with the sun's warmth on her face. With a contented sigh, she continued watching the dogs play as Tim threw a tennis ball for them. Sounds of panting, barks and excited yips filled the air. And when another woman came with two Golden Retrievers, it was game on. Tess laughed, enjoying watching the four dogs tire themselves out, while their humans all stood around making small talk.

Suddenly, Tess's phone rang, so she dug in her pocket to answer it. It was Denny.

"Hey Denny, how'd the meeting go?" she asked as the dogs came barreling past her.

"Fine," he said. "Where are you? It sounds like you're being attacked by animals or something."

"Dog park. Otter is busy playing with some friends," she smiled.

"Ahh, I see. Well, I was just calling to let you know that Miles and Scafferty are going to go to the AA meeting tonight to see if they can find out anything about Gary Hinsley. I was going to go, but they offered. I think I'll use some of that time to hang out with Natalie."

"Is she doing okay?"

"Seems to be, I guess," Denny said with a sigh. "The school has agreed to move Lainey into a different class and monitor the situation closer. Apparently Natalie isn't the only one complaining about her."

"Poor Nat. I hope this helps her and that the school actually follows through. Bullying is such a terrible situation to be stuck in."

"Agreed. I really just want to go off on Lainey's parents, but there's that whole law enforcement and 'your kid is watching you' thing going on. That makes it hard." Denny said, his voice tired.

"True, " Tess agreed. "Kids are always watching how adults react to things."

"Pretty much. Okay well, I gotta get her loaded up and put some food into her. I'll talk to you later," Denny said. Tess said goodbye and hung up, watching the dogs as they continued to play.

A few moments later, Tess's phone rang again, and she pulled it out to answer it. She smiled to herself, assuming it was Denny once again calling to pester her. But when she looked at her phone, it said 'unavailable'. A look of confusion crossed her face.

"This is Tess," she answered the phone but was met with silence. "Hello?" More silence.

"Hello? This is Tess. Can I help you?" she said, glancing back down at the phone. The call was still live, the timer counting the seconds as they passed. She put the phone back to her ear. "Who is this?"

And then she heard it—breathing. The caller remained quiet except for the gentle sound of their exhalations. Tess felt the hair on the back of her neck raise as she glanced around her. Tim and the other dog owner were deep in conversation, oblivious to the fact that Tess was frozen in fear.

"Who is this?" she said again, this time using a sterner voice. Still, nothing but breathing sounds. Tess, feeling exposed and paranoid, quickly hung up the phone. Grabbing Otter's leash, she zipped up her jacket against the October chill and called for her dog.

As Otter came bounding over to her, tennis ball in his mouth, Tess's phone rang again. Clipping the leash on the dog, Tess pulled her phone out again. Unavailable.

"Who is this?" she ground into the phone. As before, she was met with silence, except for breathing.

"Stop calling this number if you aren't going to speak," she snapped, even as she looked around, feeling vulnerable.

"Tsk, tsk, Tess," came a male voice over the phone. "No need to be rude."

"I'm not being rude. You're that one that keeps calling me and not talking. Who is this, and what do you want?" Tess said, willing herself not to sound so aggressive.

"Just a friend," the voice said. "I hope you like my work. You know, the boats, the Breaking Wheel..."

"Who are you? Why are you doing this?" she said, desperate to get some answers. The killer had made contact, but she had no way to trace the call.

"I'm not going to tell you that... yet," he said, his voice deep and smooth. "As for why I'm doing it—well, just remember this. Secrets are torture." He laughed then, a quiet, cruel laugh. "Oh, and Tess?"

"Yes?"

"I liked your coat better unzipped. The yellow sweater looks nice on you." Then the line went dead.

Thursday, October 27th, 5:30 p.m.

Immediately after the phone call from the killer, Tess called Denny and told him what had happened. As he urgently told her to get out of there and meet him at the station, Tess practically ran back home and loaded up a tired, panting Otter into her car and headed out.

Hands shaking, she drove to the sheriff's department and saw Denny waiting there for her. Natalie sat at the conference room table working on homework and eating some snacks. Her eyes lit up when she saw Tess and Otter enter the room.

Without a word, Tess handed Natalie the dog's leash and then collapsed in a chair next to where Denny was standing. He squatted down to look Tess in the eyes, taking her shaking hands in his.

"He was watching me, Denny," Tess breathed, her voice filled with fear. "I didn't see anybody, but he was definitely watching me. He had seen me zip my coat and even knew the color of my sweater!"

"The guys are working on tracing the call right now, Tess. They'll get the information to us as soon as they find out. I know it's hard, but just try to relax."

"It'll be okay, Tess," Natalie said, coming to put a small hand on Tess's knee. Tess gave the young girl a half smile, trying to calm her own fear.

Suddenly, the door opened as Detective Malone came into the room, a grim look on his face. Denny and Tess watched him expectantly.

"Sorry, guys, it appears the caller used a burner phone. Virtually untraceable."

"Well, now what?" Tess said miserably. "I won't be able to relax while someone is watching me."

"We'll have a unit watch your house tonight," Malone stated. "Surely the caller won't be so bold as to call you back. Also, you can use the feature on your phone to block all unknown numbers. If he really wants to get a hold of you, maybe he'll use a traceable phone number next time."

"God, I hope there isn't a next time," Tess said, suddenly glad she had installed a security system when her dad had suggested it.

Chapter Fifteen

Thursday, October 27th, 6:52 p.m.

Shit! Brian thought as he crammed his baseball hat lower on his head, checking the rearview mirror again. That was most definitely a cop. And now that he thought about it, two cops.

He'd gone to St. Catherines that night to attend the AA meeting. He wanted to make sure he was casually seen at the meeting he'd been attending for the past two months as he'd watched Gary Hinsley. He'd tried to insert himself into the fringes of the older man's life to learn his routine. He just wanted to avoid his sudden absence being correlated with that of Hinsley's absence, should anyone come around asking questions. Obviously, Brian had gone to the meeting the week before, even though he knew Gary wasn't going to be showing up. Gary had been "indisposed" that night, laying handcuffed and naked in boats in the yard of a deserted house at the end of the lake.

Brian had gone to the AA meeting tonight with the intention of it being his last one. He didn't even drink, so really, what was the point now? He was tired of listening to other people's sob stories about how pathetic their lives were. God. All the drama had made him almost *want* to start drinking. After he'd seen his own mother's downward spiral into drugs and alcohol, Brian had vowed to abstain from both vices.

Now, as he backed his late model Honda Civic out of the church parking lot, he kept glancing in the rearview mirror. He'd seen the two men come in together, even though they tried to act like they didn't. They looked like cops from a mile away despite them wearing street clothes. *Nice try, fellas*, Brian thought, as he quickly left the parking lot and headed toward the outskirts of town, desperate to get away. Luckily for him, he'd never actually gotten out of his car. He'd been about to when he saw them walking up the stone steps to the church. They stuck out like a sore thumb, and he'd immediately noticed them. They seemed oblivious of him, but he didn't want to take any chances.

Why were they there? What had tipped them off? Probably Gary's wife. He frowned at the thought. He should have known that the cops would have interviewed Sarah Hinsley pretty fast. They always seem to want to rule out the spouse first. Little did they know, Sarah had been married to a monster.

He knew they couldn't have put a trace on his cell phone. He'd used a burner phone from Walmart to call Tess Dane earlier, just to mess with her. He wanted to see if he could get any information from her about the case. His efforts had been futile, and his irritation had grown. The news hadn't shared a lot of details about the two murders, and the suspense was getting to Brian. Had they connected the dots yet? Was he or his mother under scrutiny?

As he headed home from the church, he made sure to deviate from his usual route, constantly looking in his mirrors. So far, no one seemed to be following him. He tried to relax but knew that he couldn't. Not yet. He'd only begun his work. He'd relax once he was finished and not a second before.

Thursday, October 27th, 8:42 p.m.

Denny was just walking out of the Swain County Sheriff's Office when his cell phone rang. Glancing at the caller ID, he answered, "Hey, Deputy Miles, how's it going? Did you find anything at St. Catherines?"

"Yes and no," Deputy Miles said with a sigh. "Scafferty and I went to the AA meeting in plain clothes. We didn't want to scare off anyone by wearing our uniforms. Only about five people showed up: two old guys, a woman with a petite frame, and two younger guys. One man was black and the other white."

"Ok. So, assuming our theory about the perp being a man because of all the heavy lifting involved with the boats and body is true, we can focus on the men at the meeting. Let's stick a pin in the woman's possible involvement for now. You said that there were two old guys? Like how old? One foot in the grave or just older than you?"

Miles chuckled, "Definitely late seventies at the youngest. They've been around for a while, but I doubt they had anything to do with this murder. Both seemed too weak to handle something like this."

"So that leaves us with the two younger guys," Denny thought aloud. "Were you able to get any info on their identities? I know it's Alcoholics Anonymous, but you never know."

"I can do better," Miles said. "Scafferty stood around taking a smoke break in the parking lot afterwards when people started to leave. He got plate numbers on both men's vehicles, while I stayed inside and waited for everyone to head out. Once I was alone with Carol Marteese, the meeting coordinator, I identified myself and tried to get some information. She seemed annoyed that I'd even asked, considering the whole 'anonymous' part."

"True. That *is* the point of AA," Denny said as he headed to his vehicle. Clicking the key fob, he unlocked the door and got in. "It was a good try though."

"I didn't say she didn't give me anything," Miles said, humor in his voice. "I said she was annoyed."

"Ok then. What did she tell you?"

"She didn't give me names or personal details for anyone, obviously. But when I told her we were investigating the homicide of a recent attendee, she seemed more keen on acknowledging my questions. Her eyes lit up in recognition when I showed her the picture of Gary Hinsley. I asked her if anyone new, specifically men in their early twenties to late fifties, had recently started to attend. If they had seemed to interact with Hinsley, in particular. She nodded and held up two fingers. I asked her if they'd been there tonight and again she nodded and held up one finger," Miles said before continuing. "I walked over to the two chairs where the young men had sat, the black guy and the white one. Then I just asked her one more question."

"Which was?" Denny pushed, excitedly.

"I placed a hand on each of their chairs and asked which one she preferred—left or right."

"And....?" Denny said hopefully, understanding where this was going.

"She said she preferred the left chair, indicating the seat where the white guy had sat."

"So, now we need to identify the white guy that was there tonight. This is the break we needed. Awesome work, you two." Denny said before ending the call.

Chapter Sixteen

Friday, October 28th, 7:55 a.m.

"Good morning, everyone," the sheriff said, beginning the morning progress meeting as people finished arriving and finding seats. As the investigation plodded forward, the officers began taking on a more sleep-deprived zombie persona; each either high on caffeine from too much coffee, or desperately trying to keep their eyes open.

"I know everyone's annoyed that we have to work over the weekend, but the media is already running with this. National news is already spreading stories about the "Boat Man," and how there is a sadistic killer loose in our county. They aren't wrong, but I still don't want Swain County getting a bad rep. We need to make progress now. If we continue to work together, both BCI and the sheriff's department will be able to stop this mess before things get more out of control. I'm surprised the mayor hasn't been on my ass over this."

"Well, sir, you'll be happy to know that we were able to make some progress last night at St. Catherines," Scafferty said, before taking a bite of his breakfast sandwich. He swallowed before saying, "I was able to get the license plates of two possible people of interest. Miles and I had gone to the AA meeting to see if there was anything to learn about Gary Hinsley. There were only a handful of people in attendance, and we quickly narrowed our attention down to two men that we may want to question. Is there a reason to believe Gary was killed by someone at AA? Not particularly, but at this stage in the investigation, we are leaving nothing to chance."

"Two of the guys were in an age bracket that more than likely would include our perp. The other men at the meeting were too old and weak to move bodies and boats around," Miles inserted. "While Scafferty watched them and took down their plate numbers, I spoke with the leader of the AA meeting. She was a woman of few words, but I was able to understand that two men had recently started attending meetings—and one of the two was there last night."

"The plates belong to James Kane and Anthony Enderle. We ran records on both men out of an abundance of caution. James Kane was squeaky clean, not even a parking ticket. Anthony Enderle, not so much," Scafferty said looking down at his notes. "Now, Carol Marteese, the meeting coordinator did indicate to Deputy Miles that the new member that was there last night was white, meaning Anthony Enderle is now under scrutiny."

"Based on what exactly?" Denny asked, confusion wrinkling his forehead. "Just because he's a white guy that recently started AA?"

"Based on the fact that Carol Marteese said Enderle and Hinsley had become pretty chatty at meetings and even went out afterwards together occasionally, which in and of itself isn't overly concerning," Miles said. "Rather typical of AA attendees actually, according to Marteese. We want to talk to Enderle because he was friendly with Gary, but also because he has a felony for assault with a deadly weapon and apparently a short fuse."

"I see, " said the sheriff. "And have you been able to make contact with Mr. Enderle?"

"Yes, sir," Scafferty said. "We got a hold of him last night, and he's agreed to come and speak with us. He'll be here around eleven."

"Good work, Miles, Sacafferty," the sheriff then turned to Claybourne. "Any news on the boats? Where did they come from?"

"Well sir, I've contacted the marinas in the area, and no one sells, refurbishes, or stores wooden boats like the ones found at Lake Amelia. Most wooden boats can last twenty-five to thirty years or more if they are taken care of. The two from the scene obviously weren't. I'd guess they were newer than that, but I can't seem to find if they were bought here or brought from somewhere else."

"I think I may be able to help with that," Officer Miles inserted. He looked around the table and then at the sheriff. "Scafferty and I were asked to canvas the houses around Lake Amelia. Our efforts were to determine if anyone had seen or heard any suspicious activity during the days leading up to the discovery of the man in the boats. We didn't find anyone who knew anything. Most of the houses are already winterized, and the owners are away for the season. We made some calls to the ones we could locate and asked them if they had any security cameras on site or remote access that they could review. Most of the houses have either docks or boat houses. The public docks at the lake don't allow for boats to be in the water year-round, so most have already pulled out and have them in storage."

"We did find an older couple that has a weekend cabin at the far end of the lake. No security. When we asked about missing boats, the man said he had three rowboats laying near his woodline, and that over the summer two of them had gone missing. He just chalked it up to unruly teens and chose to move on. He said they were old and unused as his kids were grown and never came to visit the lake anymore."

"Perfect," Burrows said as Claybourne approached the white board and began writing down the name of the old couple, their address, and other pertinent information.

"Did they say when the boats went missing? May help us narrow down the dates for residents to check their security footage," Malone suggested.

"Already on it," Scafferty piped in. "Mr. Boggs, the owner of the missing boats, said when they visited the cabin at the end of September, the boats were there. When they came back to the house two weeks ago, they were gone. We have the community homeowners looking for suspicious activity or the boats from September 27th until last Wednesday when the body was found."

"We know Gary Hinsley was found Wednesday morning but was missing in action since the Thursday before," Denny commented. "Hopefully somebody sees something on their footage."

"What? Like some deranged killer is just putzing around the lake with a stiff in the back?" Malone said sarcastically. "If anything, he waited until cover of darkness, grabbed the boats, and put them in a trailer or something."

"Or he just took Hinsley to the Boggs' cabin and used their shed or dock for his work," Tess said. "Why lug two stolen boats out on a trailer when anyone could see you? Wouldn't it make more sense to just take the victim to the boats? Tied up in the trunk or just drugged when they got there?"

"True. If I was going to be doing the boat thing, I think I'd get my victim as close as I could to the scene. Less chance I'd be seen and less lifting. I mean, a rowboat weighs what? A hundred, two hundred pounds each? Work smarter not harder," Malone said, doodling in the margin of his notes.

"The Boggs' cabin was at the end of the lake? Rather deserted, you'd say?" Tess asked Officer Miles. He nodded. Tess thought for a second. "It makes sense. Deserted end of the lake, wait until dark, empty house. Take your victim there and stick him in the boats."

"But what about the timing?" Denny wondered. "Didn't you say that a person being executed by way of The Boats could live for days? Our perp would have had to have kept Gary in the boats somewhere until he died and then shoved him into the lake, right? Why risk all that trouble, just to have Gary bobbing around still alive and being found too early?"

"All good points," Tess said. Their theories all sounded plausible, but which one was the right one?

Denny took in all the information, making notes to himself as he went, "Good work guys. We've made progress. That should make the mayor happy."

Chapter Seventeen

Friday, October 28th, 11:27 a.m.

"Thanks for coming down, Mr. Enderle, " Denny said, sliding into a chair across from the man who'd been at the AA meeting the night before.

"Sure, " he mumbled, looking around nervously. "What did you need to ask me? The cop last night said it had something to do with Gary from AA?"

"That's right," Denny said, pulling a photo of Gary Hinsley out of his stack of papers. "Is this the man you know as Gary?" Enderle nodded and Denny continued. "This is Gary Hinsley. He was found dead early Wednesday morning. Murdered." He watched Enderle closely for any reaction.

"Murdered?" Enderle said, genuine shock filling his face. Tess watched the man's face as well, scrutinizing his mannerisms. Either he was a top-notch actor, or he was seriously surprised to hear about Gary.

"Unfortunately, yes," Tess inserted, "He was found down at Lake Amelia."

"Wait, the guy in the boat?" Enderle asked incredulously, "That was Gary? Oh my God. This is so fucked up." He rubbed his stubbled chin with his hand and looked up at the ceiling for a moment to collect himself.

"How well did you know Gary Hinsley?" Denny asked after a moment. A pause, the only sound in the room was that of the clicking clock over the door.

"Some, I'd say," Enderle finally replied, picking at a cuticle. Tess noticed that the man's leg began to nervously bob up and down under the table.

"When was the last time you saw Gary?" Denny asked, looking down at his notes for a moment before going on, "At AA or somewhere else?"

"You don't think I did it do you?" Enderle asked suddenly, panic beginning to fill his voice. "Is that why y'all call me in here? Am I under arrest?" He began to shove away from the table in a rush, but Tess moved around toward the door, hoping to deter him for a few moments.

"No, Anthony," Denny said, "You aren't under arrest. We are just asking questions. We know that Gary went to St. Catherine's once a week for the AA meetings. We are just trying to feel around for any information he may have shared that would help us find his killer." Enderle seemed to relax, although marginally, and nodded for Denny to proceed.

"Do you know of anyone who may have had something against Gary? Anything he ever talked about?"

"Like all of us at AA, we have a past," Enderle said, leaning back in his chair. "Some of it we share, some we don't. Gary wasn't really a sharer. He was quiet at first but then as the meetings progressed he seemed to open up. All I remember him saying was that he'd done things in his past he wasn't proud of."

"Don't we all," Tess said. She thought for a moment, "We know about your felony, Anthony." She held up her hands to calm him when he balked, "I'm only bringing it up to see if perhaps Gary ever mentioned going to prison, or ever being questioned by law enforcement himself."

Tess watched Enderle processing her question. With a shrug, he said, "I told the group about being in prison as part of my twelve steps. I am on step five: admitting my bad deeds to myself, my peers, and my god."

"And was Gary also on step five?" Denny asked, "Did he tell you or the group as a whole anything of importance?"

Enderle shook his head, "He was past that. What he did was include me into the group. Listened to my story, let me just....talk things through. It was really what I needed.

A friend." He sniffed and tried to hide it with a shrug. "He said, 'You can't change your past, no matter how much you try, but you can change your future with hard work and good decisions.' I try to live by that."

"Sounds like Gary really made an impact on you, huh?" Tess said with a wistful smile. "Did you ever see anybody else talking to him while he was hanging around the church for meetings?"

"He was friendly with everybody, really," Enderle said, rubbing his hand over his close-cropped hair. "There was another newer guy that would sit with us. He said his name was John. Who knows if that's his real name or not. A lot of people at AA meetings don't use their real names, you know? Well anyway, Gary would talk to John a lot too."

"Did you like John like you did Gary?"

"No, not really," Enderle said, looking from Tess to Denny and then back to Tess. "He wasn't really that friendly to me. Acted like I wasn't there which is fine by me. I wasn't there to make friends really, and I don't think he was either."

"Can you tell us what John looked like?"

"Sure, I guess. He was taller than me by a couple of inches, so maybe.....6 foot 2? I think he was probably in his early to mid twenties, but I've never been good at guessing people's ages. He was an average guy with dark brown hair," Enderle said. "Why? You think he did that to Gary? The news said the body was in a boat and mutilated?"

"At this point in the investigation, we are just asking around and getting information. We aren't accusing anyone of anything," Tess said, watching Enderle closely. "Is there anything else you can think of that could prove helpful?"

"Not that I can think of, no."

"And just to check for our records, where were you the night of October 23rd?

"The same place I am most nights," Enderle stated. "I'm a cook down at Ida's Diner. I work the night shift—9 p.m. to 5 a.m. I don't work the breakfast rush unless I have to fill in for somebody. You can check with Lisa, the shift manager. She'll vouch for me."

"Ok. Well, thank you for your time, for coming down here and answering our questions," Denny said, standing and shaking Anthony Enderle's hand. "If you think of anything or hear anything that may be helpful, just reach out." He handed Enderle a business card before they said their goodbyes and escorted him to the door.

Chapter Eighteen

Saturday, October 29th, 8:37 a.m.

The morning dawned bright and early with a coolness in the air. Bethany Potter stepped out on her back stoop to watch Gigi, her Yorkie, run around the backyard to find the perfect place to relieve herself. Steaming cup of coffee in hand, Bethany tried to ignore the nagging feeling in the back of her mind.

Her husband hadn't come home again last night, just like the night previous. He hadn't even bothered to return her calls. He'd pulled this crap on her before, back a few years ago. Of course, he'd said he was working on his campaign and that "running for mayor was serious business." She'd later find out that, yes, he was working on his campaign all right—his campaign manager, Kimberly Francis, that is.

Bethany pulled a face now as she thought back to her husband's indiscretions. A bark of laughter escaped her lips just thinking about it. Little Kimmy Francis (with her perky breasts, flat stomach, and bubbly personality) wasn't the only woman who'd led her husband astray. Bethany wasn't an idiot. She knew Corey would screw anything that looked his way.

She groaned, instantly in a foul mood. Where was he? The girls had their cheer competition at ten, but they needed to be there by nine thirty.

"I swear to God, he better not make us late again today," she grumbled to herself. Corey, her husband of nearly fifteen years, was chronically late, if he even bothered to show up at all. Bethany truly could care less at this point in their marriage. She poured her energy into raising their three daughters, caring for their large home on the better side of town. Other than having a cheating husband, Bethany Potter lived a charmed life: PTO mom, successful work from home job that allowed her to be involved with her children's lives, a large circle of friends, singing in the church choir every Sunday, and driving a brand-new Infiniti QX80 SUV.

Even now, as she watched her dog work on a bowel movement, she found that despite Corey's infidelities, she was content. Yes, she wished he'd have the courtesy to call her or even come home at night. But, as long as he was kind to the girls, and provided for their family, she was content enough to turn a blind eye to his behaviors.

Gigi wiped her feet off in the dewy grass and then bounded up the steps to Bethany's feet. The woman bent to scoop up the little dog and then headed into the house.

Bethany set the dog down and picked up her phone. Still no texts from Corey. With a sigh, she called his phone yet again, but it just rang through to voicemail. Sighing, she left a message for him to call her as soon as he could, and then hanging up, she called his office. It was nearly 9:00 a.m., but surely someone would be there. The city didn't stop for the weekend which meant Corey didn't either.

Her call rang through and then after a moment, a voice answered.

"Mayor's office, this is Kimmy." A perky voice came over the phone. Bethany rolled her eyes.

"Hi, Kimmy. Is Corey in?" she said impatiently.

"No, Mrs. Potter," Kimmy said, her voice losing most of its cheerfulness. "He isn't in yet today and he wasn't in yesterday or Thursday either. He's supposed to be having a special weekend meeting today with Mr. Temple, the architect for the Sheridan building downtown."

"Really?" Bethany responded as concern filled her being. She hadn't seen her husband since... Wednesday morning? It was Saturday morning now, cheerleading day at the high school. Had her husband really not been at home or work since he left home Wednesday morning? Surely not.

"No, Mrs. Potter," Kimmy said again. "He was here Wednesday morning, said he had one of his headaches. But then he got a phone call and left quickly afterwards. I just assumed he didn't come back after lunch because of his head."

"Do you know who called him?" Bethany asked, a feeling of dread coursing through her.

"Not that I recall. Hang on a sec," Kimmy said. Bethany could hear papers being shuffled around as though Kimmy was looking for something. "Ok, I found my note. I always make a note of who comes or calls at the office. My mother says I'm weird like that."

Bethany did not want to discuss Kimmy's mother, or if the young woman was weird. She just wanted to find her husband. *Where was he?*

"What does the note say, Kim?" Bethany said, trying to call the woman back to task.

"Ummm... looks like the call came in around 10:45 a.m. Some guy... said his name was Brad or Brian, no last name. Demanded to talk to Mr. Potter immediately,"

Kimmy said. "Kind of rude, if I remember correctly, like he wouldn't take no for an answer."

"Thanks Kimmy. You've been very helpful," Bethany said. After ending the call, she immediately phoned the police.

Chapter Nineteen

Saturday, October 29th, 9:23 a.m.

"So, you think this lunatic is going around, torturing innocent men, just for kicks?" Malone asked, making a face.

The group had reconvened in the conference room, each with a cup of coffee or tea in front of them. They all looked exhausted. It had been long hours the previous day, and today looked as though it would be the same.

"It's just a theory, sir," Tess said. She'd just presented her findings about the Breaking Wheel, and much to the dismay of her colleagues, she had a feeling she was on the right track. "I don't think it's just for kicks though. It's too graphic, too... personal, almost like revenge for something."

"So, we've got Gary Hinsley, killed via The Boats, and now a John Doe via the Breaking Wheel. First off, how the hell did people even come up with these ways of punishment?" Sheriff Burrows said, running a hand through his thinning gray hair. "The depravity of the times."

"We, as a species, haven't changed much, sir," Claybourne commented. Burrows nodded in resigned agreement.

"So, if they killed criminals and guilty people like this back in medieval times, should we assume that these truly *are* revenge killings?" Malone said before taking a sip of his coffee. "For example, maybe the perp thinks that the vics got away with something in the past? Or they weren't punished enough?"

"I'd have to agree with Malone," Denny said, glancing at everyone in turn. "These murders are overkill. You can shoot somebody who pisses you off easily. Sure, it's still wrong and at the end of the day the victim is still dead. But going through all the planning, logistics, execution—pun not intended—and the torture before death seems to make them extremely personal."

Heads nodded around the table. "Unfortunately, I think you're right," Burrows said. "We can't let the media get wind of this. They would have a field day! And just wait until the mayor hears about this. He's going to be breathing down our necks to get this thing solved." He turned to Mike Seawell. "Any new evidence from last night that will help us catch this son of a bitch?"

"Well, Sir, as Deputy Dane pointed out, our John Doe was strapped to the water wheel down at the old mill. I don't believe that is where he was actively tortured though. My technicians found an old timey wagon wheel, you know, like from one of those Conestoga wagons from the Oregon Trail? Well, we found one discarded in the weeds behind the water wheel in a large amount of blood and disturbed dirt. Someone had taken the time to pound nails into the wooden wheel and out through the metal rim. Pretty barbaric, if you ask me. The nails and rim were covered in blood. Preliminary tests showed it was human blood. We'll have to wait for the lab to confirm it was from our vic, but we all know the probability is high that it is." Seawell paused to review his notes quickly. "As I already told Detective Haywood, the wagon wheel had a partial fingerprint. I had one of my guys run it through AFIS. It was too smudged to be useful.."

"What about the footprints in the mud? Are they a match for the other crime scene?" Malone asked.

Seawell nodded, "We took plaster casts of the impressions, as well as photographs. They appear to be similar to the ones found at the original scene, but my techs will continue to compare the two later today to confirm. From what we know so far, I would say, with some certainty, that we are dealing with the same killer or killers."

"What about the body itself on the water wheel? Like, if he was already dead, why stick him on the wagon wheel?" Denny wondered aloud.

"Perhaps just to make him suffer more until he died?" Tess offered. "Imagine. He drags his victim to the mill, makes him strip, beats the hell out of him with the spiked wheel, breaking his legs, arms, face, whatever in the process but the guy is still alive. So, the perp drags him up to the water wheel, ties him up by what's left of his arms and legs, and then emasculates him, leaving him to die a painful and miserable death," she paused, glancing back at the men who were all staring at her. "What?"

"That's some pretty messed up shit," Claybourne said. "You make that up on the fly?"

"Well... yeah. It wasn't that hard," Tess said, giving them a look. "Do *you* have any other scenarios you'd like to share with the group?" After a moment of silence from Claybourne, she mumbled, "Thought so."

"Has anyone heard from Dr. Summers yet?" Sheriff Burrows asked, changing the subject. Claybourne wouldn't look at Tess, so she rolled her eyes. Men.

"She said she'd be finishing up the autopsy of the Water Wheel John Doe this morning and would forward her findings on as soon as possible," Denny said.

Just then, the door opened and Bertie, the receptionist for the past forty years, stuck her head in the room. "I'm sorry to interrupt, sir," she said. When the sheriff nodded, she continued.

"We just got a call from the mayor—"

"Mary, Mother of Jesus, that didn't take long," huffed Burrows, cutting the woman off. "I was hoping that he wouldn't hear about all this mess to buy us time to figure out who's responsible!"

"But sir—"

"What, Bertie? Spit it out."

"It's not the mayor himself, sir. It's his wife," Bertie said, holding up a piece of paper with a handwritten message hastily scrawled on it. "It seems that he's missing."

Chapter Twenty

Saturday, October 29th, 10:15 a.m.

"Thanks for coming in to speak to us, Mrs. Potter," Denny said, offering her a bottle of water and a seat. Tess stood over to the side watching as the mayor's wife took the water and sat down in one of the plush chairs in the sheriff's office. "I'm Detective Haywood. This is Deputy Tess Dane." The two women exchanged mumbled pleasantries.

"So, you wanted to report your husband missing?" Denny asked as he sat behind the sheriff's desk with a pen and paper in his hand.

"Yes. Yes, that's right," Bethany Potter said, a look of worry etched into her pretty face. Tess watched her silently as the older woman pushed her long blonde hair over her lean shoulders with a well-manicured hand.

"What makes you think that he's missing?" Denny asked, closely observing the worried woman in front of him.

"Well, because I haven't seen him since he left for work Wednesday morning. His receptionist said that she saw him at work that morning, so I know he made it to work." She paused a moment in thought. "Kimmy, the receptionist, said that he'd been complaining of a headache. Around 10:45, a call came through for him. She said that the man on the phone was rather pushy, demanding to speak with my husband. Apparently Corey eventually took the phone call, and moments later he abruptly left. He hasn't been seen at work since then, and he hasn't been home."

Denny raised his eyebrows in concern then thought for a few seconds. "Any idea who called him?"

"No," Bethany said thoughtfully. "Kimmy said the man's name was Brad or Brian. Something like that. She couldn't remember exactly."

"Do you or your husband know anyone by either of those names?"

"No, not that I can think of."

Denny scrawled some notes to himself. "Pretty much everyone around here knows what your husband looks like so we will keep an eye out. Does he have any distinguishing marks, piercings, tattoos, mannerisms? What kind of car does he drive?"

"He drives a black Tesla," Bethany said, a worried look clouding her features. "He doesn't have scars or birthmarks, no piercings either." She thought for a moment. "He does have a tattoo though... on his chest. Some kind of bird with flames coming out of it or something. I don't know what kind. I've never liked it."

Denny caught Tess's eye and then looked back at Bethany. He pulled out the close-up photo of Gary Hinsley's tattoo and laid it on the desk. Sliding it toward Bethany Potter he asked, "Does it look anything like this?"

Bethany leaned forward, looking at the photo. "Yes. Almost exactly. How did you know that?" She looked up at Denny and then Tess, her face desperate for answers. "Where did you get that? Where is my husband?" her voice coming in a wave of panic.

"Mrs. Potter, please... remain calm. We are only asking questions," Denny asked, reaching for the photo.

"Is that person dead? Is my husband dead?" The shrillness of Bethany's voice filled the room.

"This tattoo was found on a victim of a recent crime." Denny said gently. Bethany began to sob, knowing what Denny was about to say but hoping that he wouldn't. "When you described the tattoo your husband has, it sounded like this one. We are trying to track down where it came from. Perhaps your husband got his at the same tattoo parlor? Do you know where he went to get his?"

Bethany's sobs slowly quieted as she realized that the person in the picture was not her husband after all, and that maybe somehow, he was still going to come home.

"Corey never liked to talk about the tattoo. All I know is that he got it when he was really young," she replied as she thought for a moment. "You know, I do remember him saying it was symbolic of rising above his past mistakes. He said that a friend did it for him."

"Any idea what friend?" Denny gently pressed. Tess could tell that he was hoping for more information, but there was a nagging thought in the back of her brain. Their John Doe from the old mill, could he be Corey Potter, the mayor of Camden Town? Surely not. Who would want the mayor dead? And why?

"No, not really," Bethany said. "I think it was from his college days, maybe even high school. That was so long ago. Maybe... twenty five or thirty years ago now?"

"What high school did your husband attend?" Denny asked her. Tess watched as the woman took a drink from her bottle of water.

"Why does this matter?" she asked. "My husband is missing and you're wanting to talk about some tattoo he got in high school? Unbelievable." She shook her head as she wiped at her eyes.

"Ma'am, with all due respect, we *are* trying to find your husband. It just also happens that there was a man murdered a few days ago that had the same tattoo as your husband. I'm not accusing him, or you, of anything," Denny said, sounding frustrated. "I am just trying to determine a link, if any, between your husband and the murdered man."

Bethany hung her head in shame at her outburst. "I'm sorry. This is just so scary for me. I just want my husband home."

"I can understand that," Denny said softly. He handed her a box of tissues.

"Sherman Hills," Bethany said as she softly blew her nose. At Denny's slightly confused expression, she added. "His school... he graduated from Sherman Hills."

"The prep school near Columbus?" Tess asked. Bethany nodded.

Once they were through with questioning Bethany Potter and gathering information to aid in finding her husband, Denny made two phone calls. The first was to the head mistress of Sherman Hills Preparatory School. He had to leave a message since it was a Saturday, which meant the school office was closed. He requested an appointment for early Monday and left his call back number.

He then called Dr. Summers office to schedule a time to talk with her about the autopsy results. He and Tess were suspicious now that the man in the morgue was none other than Mayor Corey Potter.

Chapter Twenty-One

Saturday, October 29th, 2:45 p.m.

Around mid-afternoon, Denny and Tess stopped in to chat with Dr. Summers about her findings. She was almost done with her work as she'd put a rush on it, even coming in to work on a Saturday. The quicker they ID'd this guy, the quicker they ID'd the perp. As she worked, Denny filled Abby in on the events of the morning.

"So, we think this is the mayor?" she asked, looking up from the open chest cavity she was working on. Her face shield flashed reflections of the corpse from the light of the overhead fixtures.

"It fits. I don't want to think that, but it fits," Tess said, leaning in slightly to look inside the remains. Most of the organs had already been removed, leaving an empty hollow space. "According to his wife, he hasn't been seen since early Wednesday morning, and he also has the phoenix tattoo."

Abby seemed to think about it for a moment, and then shrugged. "You could be on to something. The height and age fit, even the tattoo. Too bad his face is so messed up. If it wasn't we could use it to ID him officially. I'll have to send some DNA to the lab for a conclusive ID which as you know can take some time. I'm not about to ask his wife to look at that." She nodded toward the pulpy mess of flesh that had once been the man's face.

Denny sighed. He hated this part. "I guess we'll have to go tell Bethany Potter of our suspicions."

Saturday, October 29th, 7:00 p.m.

Later that evening, the sheriff called an emergency progress meeting and demanded that everyone show up. With the mayor as a potential victim, Burrows was trying to avoid a media shit storm; and everyone knew it. There would be a public outcry if they were unable to solve this case and stop the gruesome killings. Routine murders, if there were such a thing, rarely happened in the Camden and Crawley area. Columbus sure, but not small-town

Ohio. Having not one but two murders involving torture and abuse of a corpse within a 48-hour period of time was just unheard of.

Right at 7:00 p.m., the detectives and officers involved in the case began filing into their usual conference room at the end of the hall. Some looked annoyed, some exhausted, while others seemed strangely optimistic.

Tess was one of the strangely optimistic ones. She'd been researching various torture and execution methods through the ages and had gone down a dark rabbit hole of information. She'd made notes about The Boats method as well at The Breaking Wheel method, hoping that something would stand out and crack the case. The killer, while inflicting the punishments, seemed to add his own flare on things. The emasculations were one difference from historical examples. Unsure of where exactly that fit into the scheme of things, Tess was sure it was important.

"Alright folks, settle down," the sheriff commanded, the room instantly quieting. "First things first. I know the major question on everyone's mind is who the man on the Breaking Wheel is. It seems that there is a strong probability that the guy on the wheel is Mayor Potter."

A murmur of voices filled the room, questions bombarding the sheriff. He held his hands up to shush them. "Now, obviously, we don't want the media to hear about this, so keep it close to the chest. Mrs. Potter has been told, and Officer Kennedy, the liaison, is there at the house with them as they journey through this process. We will be holding a press conference tomorrow morning to address the mayor's absence and our findings. Tonight though, we are giving Mrs. Potter time to mourn and be with her children. I'm sure you all can understand." He paused, looking around the table at each person in turn.

"Now, this morning our meeting was interrupted, and we didn't get a chance to go over everyone's findings. Anyone else have anything to contribute? Updates on the surveillance at the lake?"

"You beat me to it, Sheriff," Claybourne said, with a nod at Burrows. "I have received a couple of calls and emails from residents that have properties around Lake Amelia. Now, remember the Boggs family was the older couple that owns the house with the missing boats." He stood then, approached the whiteboard, and taped up an 8X10 map of Lake Amelia. Taking a red marker, he circled a house on the lake's south end. "This is the Boggs' place. And here is the home of Royce Taylor." He circled another property.

"Royce Taylor? That lawyer guy on TV with the cheesy commercials?" Malone laughed. Claybourne nodded.

"Yep, one and the same," Claybourne answered. "He contacted us via email. He'd attached a rather grainy video from the evening of October 23rd. I've seen the video clip, and I'm not too excited. The video was taken at night, around 1:15 a.m. and the weather was rainy and windy. Visibility is bad, but there is a small boat seen making its way past the Taylors' dock. Because of the camera's angle, only the bottom half of the boat appears on the screen. You can't see any oars or people in it, just the bottom half of the boat." He turned back to the table, referring to his notes.

"Here," he said, circling another property on the lake's shore, this time closer to where Hinsley's body had been found, "is the lake house of a woman by the name of Patricia Connelly. She's been in Rome the past month or so but was gracious enough to check her video feeds. And this is where we make some progress." He grinned and then pulled up a video on his laptop. Enlarging it as much as possible, he hit 'PLAY', and the group of officers leaned in to watch.

The date and time stamp on the video said Sunday, October 23rd, 1:29 a.m., the same night as the other video. Miss Connelly's video showed the same rain and wind as Royce Taylor's, but she had apparently spent a little more on her surveillance system. The picture quality was much better and as the group of investigators watched, a boat appeared on screen. A small metal dinghy, powered by a small motor, was towing a boat—make that two boats, one stacked on the other.

When the investigators saw the stacked boats, a collective gasp filled the air as they each leaned in further to watch. The dinghy was operated by one person—thin, tall, and wearing all black, including a zippered sweatshirt with the hood pulled up, obscuring their face. For just a second, a partial face, mostly a forehead, flashed in the darkness as the hooded figure glanced over their shoulder at the boats being tugged behind. And then the boats moved off screen.

"Well, we can't tell much about the perp, but that is definitely the boats. We have the body dump caught on tape which is great," the sheriff said. "I just wish the bastard would have looked up!"

"Agreed," Denny said, watching as the video played in a loop. "Were we able to enhance this any?" he asked hopefully, even though he was pretty sure they wouldn't be able to do much.

"Unfortunately, this is the best we are going to get. It was too dark, and the weather was crappy. We can determine that the person has light skin and an athletic physique. Not as great as a "Hello My Name is Crazy

Killer" sign, but it's at least something," Claybourne commented.

"What does the AA guy look like again?" Malone asked, looking around for any photo of Anthony Enderle. "If he looks anything like the guy in the boat, then maybe the video isn't worthless."

"They are similar enough," Scaffterty said, pulling a printout of Enderle's driver's license photo from his notes. He passed it around the table for the others to see. Anthony Enderle did, in fact, have pale skin and a lean look about him.

Chapter Twenty-Two

Saturday, October 29th, 11:30 p.m.

Late Saturday night, after taking Otter on a long walk and then soaking in the tub with a book, Tess found herself all tucked into bed. She'd just gotten into a deep sleep when her phone rang on the nightstand next to her. Jolted awake, she sat up and grabbed the phone intending on silencing it and going back to sleep. But a groggy glance at the screen changed her mind.

"Hello, this is Tess," she said, her anxiety rising.

"Hello Miss Dane. This is Angela, over at Tolliver Care Home."

"Oh. Hi, Angela. Is everything all right?"

"I'm sorry to call so late, but there was an incident tonight—with your father."

"What kind of incident?" Tess asked, her mind racing. "Is he okay?"

"He's sedated now. We aren't sure what exactly set him off earlier. He was fine one minute, watching the news with the other residents, when he started yelling and panicking."

"Oh no. How horrible! You're sure he's okay now?"

"Yes. When the orderlies tried to calm him, he started throwing punches, yelling something like, 'Make them pay! Make them pay!'" Angela said, her voice low and soothing, even if her words were not. "Needless to say, he had to be restrained. He's been given some light sedatives, but he's asking for you. He says he won't sleep until you come. I don't know what to do, Miss Dane."

"I can be there in 30 minutes," Tess said, her hand on her forehead as tears threatened to fall. She ended the call and was out the door in a matter of seconds.

Twenty-eight minutes and three red lights later, Tess pulled into the parking lot of Tolliver Care Home. Visiting hours were long gone, and the lot was mostly empty except for a handful of cars. Parking near the door and waiting to get buzzed in, Tess worried about her dad. He was all she had left in the world. She didn't count her mother; the woman had made it perfectly clear on multiple occasions that she didn't want Tess in her life.

The door buzzed, and Tess walked in. Angela greeted her with a kind smile.

"I'm so sorry to ask you to come down this late."

"It's no problem," Tess said honestly. "I'm glad you called. I'm just worried about him."

"I know, I know. We all are," Angela said as they made their way down the hall to Tommy Dane's room. "He's a favorite around here, that's for sure."

Tess smiled wistfully, thinking of better days. "Yeah, he is—was—a great dad." As they approached her father's room, they found the door partially closed and the interior light dimmed. Tess looked at Angela for guidance, and the woman nodded to go on in.

Pushing open the door gently, she found her father lying in bed, dozing. A small television was playing late night reruns, the sound muted. The small lamp beside the bed was on, casting a warm glow around the bed and side table. Otherwise, the room was shrouded in darkness. Careful not to disturb her sleeping father, she crept to his bedside, pulled a chair close and sat down.

She watched the gentle rise and fall of his chest, her heart warming to see him so relaxed. Toward the end, before he had to go into care, he was in a constant state of confusion and anxiety. He would sleep a lot. And when he was awake, he'd pace and fret. Those were the hardest days for Tess—seeing her father, once proud and strong, slipping away from her.

"Bug? Is that you?" His voice caught her off guard, and she smiled at the endearment.

"Yeah, Dad, it's me," she said, leaning closer to him. He'd opened his eyes and was looking at her, lucid and alert. "How have you been?"

"Oh, you know. Living the life," his blue eyes twinkled. "You sneak in any cookies for me?" he asked in a stage whisper.

"Of course," she whispered back with a smile, pulling out a small baggie containing three of the cookies she'd baked for Natalie.

"Good girl," he winked at her. He opened the bag, pulled one out, and held it to his mouth. As he bit off a bite and began to chew, he closed his eyes and sighed.

"What have you been up to, Tess?" her father asked as he chewed quietly.

"Well, they've partnered me with Denny again. We are working on a case together," she answered, leery of offering too much information that may stress her father out.

"Oh, you're on to detective work now?" he said smiling. "That's my girl. I knew you weren't meant to stay passing out speeding tickets your whole career." She knew he didn't mean it as an insult and smiled warmly at him.

"I guess all the hours spent reading Nancy Drew and Hardy Boys are finally paying off," she said, reaching out to rest her hand on his. His skin was cool to the touch and when he turned his hand over and lightly squeezed hers in response, she felt tears threatening to fall.

"How are you feeling tonight?" she asked, unsure if he even remembered what had happened earlier. He looked at her as he took another bite of the cookie.

"I've been better," he studied her for a moment. "I feel a little off though."

"Dad, the nurses said you got upset tonight, while watching TV. Do you remember that at all?"

"It was the news. I was watching the news." he said, another bite of cookie going into his mouth.

"They said you were shouting to 'make them pay'. Do you know what you meant by that?" Tess didn't know how much longer she'd have to get him to talk before he slipped away from her again. She was just trying to understand and see where she could help.

"They need to pay," her father said, watching her. "They didn't pay then but they are now. He knows but he's not saying."

"Dad? What are you talking about?" Tess asked, confused. He'd looked away now, staring into the corner at nothing. "Dad? Who knows?"

He turned back to her, and his lips started to quiver. He shook his head. "Who are you? Get out of my room! You don't belong here!" He threw the bag of cookies at her. "Who are you? Go away! My daughter will kick you out!"

Tears streamed down her cheeks as Tess stood and headed toward the door. She nearly ran into Angela who had come running. As Tess began running down the hall, she could still hear him yelling, "Get out! Who was that?"

Heartbroken, she made it to her car, got in and locked the door before the real tears came. She shook as the sobs racked her body, her breath coming in difficult gasps. He had forgotten who she was before, but it never got any easier. She'd learned early on, when his disease had progressed far enough to go into the care home, that the more she tried to make him remember who she was, the worse it made the situation. He'd get scared and start fighting and crying. It was the worst feeling in the world, but it was her truth and her life, whether she liked it or not.

Chapter Twenty-Three

Sunday, October 30th, 8:45 p.m.

Sunday passed uneventfully. No new bodies had been found, but the team still was no closer to finding the killer. With two men viciously murdered there was no time to waste before he may strike again. Tess spent most of the day rereading the case file, researching different topics, and spending time with Otter.

"Heaven help me, if anybody ever looks at my search history, Otter," she told the dog that Sunday evening, as he lay at her feet watching her work on her computer. He just looked up at her with weary brown eyes and yawned, his long tongue sticking out and then curling on the end.

He sighed, stood up, and made his way to his water bowl and, taking a loud, slobbery drink, ignored Tess.

"Well, okay. Fine, don't talk to me," Tess said, smiling at the dog before turning back to her computer screen. She was currently looking at Sherman Hills Prep's website in anticipation of tomorrow's visit. Clicking on the 'About Us' tab, she scrolled through the school's noble history of academic excellence. Rolling her eyes, she continued scrolling. She found the "Faculty" tab and clicked. The screen loaded, showing different department heads and faculty members. Tess noticed that a majority of the teachers were younger, with ten years or less of experience. Chewing on her bottom lip, she wondered if visiting Sherman Hills would just lead them to another dead end.

They needed to talk to faculty and staff that had been there thirty years or so ago when Corey Potter and Gary Hinsley had graced their halls as students. She sighed but continued to scroll, clicking on the 'Extracurriculars' tab. Photographs of students working on various projects, hanging out with friends, and cheering on school athletes filled her page. She clicked on a few out of curiosity but felt she was really getting nowhere. Noticing a tab that said 'Alumni', she clicked it. As it loaded, various photos popped up with small blurbs about some of the past students—basically, a brag board for future students. Tess clicked on a few random ones, seeing if there would be anything of interest to their case. Scrolling through, she read some aloud even though Otter had officially decided to abandon her by stretching out in his bed.

"How about these, Otter? Rajesh Patel, Class of 1998, doctor of cardiac surgery; Patrick Means, Class of 2003, dentist; Cristina Hopenhauer, master's in chemical engineering with a minor in avionics and integrated systems. Okay, Cristina, thanks for making me feel stupid," Tess muttered to herself as she continued to scroll through all the degrees and accolades of Sherman Hills alumni.

Finally, a name and photo caught her eye. Corey Potter, class of 1998, mayor of Camden Town and future gubernatorial candidate. Tess clicked on the link and watched as the website loaded Corey Potter's claim to fame. The blurb discussed his father's mayoral race back in 1995, and how it was Corey's dream to follow in his father's footsteps in the future by possibly running for governor. It went on to discuss Potter's academic journey and extracurriculars.

He had been on both the lacrosse and swim teams as well as various school clubs. Noticing a photo from senior year, Tess clicked on it. A photo of Corey and another boy that Tess didn't recognize stood next to the school's pool, smiling at the camera. Both were topless, clad only in swimsuits, their hair wet and spiky. Large smiles were plastered on their faces. What disturbed Tess the most was that on each of their chests there was a crudely done tattoo of a phoenix.

Chapter
Twenty-Four

Monday, October 31st, 9:34 a.m.

"So, you're saying there was no information on the other kid in the picture?" Denny asked as they pulled out of the Tim Hortons parking lot with hot coffee and some doughnut holes. They were on their way to speak to the Sherman Hills headmistress, Mrs. Nora Rodriguez-Bates. She'd called Denny first thing that morning, urgent to get the matter discussed and over with as quickly as possible. Image was everything, and even though Tess and Denny were going to just be discussing possible students from decades ago, the headmistress was eager to have the police away from school grounds as quickly as possible.

"Nope. It was like the whole bio was only for Corey," Tess said, popping a chocolate glazed doughnut hole in her mouth and chewing. After she swallowed she added, "What I thought was strange was that in some of the other alumni's bios, all the people were identified. Most were doctors, lawyers, and politicians. That kind of thing. The kid I saw had no name listed. You don't think they'd be that elitist that they'd skip over his name if he hadn't been as successful as the others?"

"I hope not. That's pretty messed up if that's the case," Denny said, turning onto Interstate 70 headed toward Columbus. They had a while before they got to the school, on the outskirts of the city, and Denny had planned well so they didn't have to rush. For that, Tess was grateful. She hated to be late.

"He had the same tattoo and everything."

"And you don't think it was Gary Hinsley?"

"No, not unless Gary had major plastic surgery and a total hair replacement. Gary was blonde and pale. This kid had a long straight nose, dark hair, tanned skin. No way it was the same kid."

"Shit," Denny said, deep in thought. "If the men are all connected somehow by that tattoo, that means there could be other victims out there. Or that someone else's life is still in danger. We have to find out who that kid is."

Nearly an hour and a half later, Denny and Tess found themselves sitting in the office of the headmistress at Sherman Hills. Mrs. Rodriguez-Bates sat at her desk while looking the two officers over. The stern looking woman, with her gray hair pulled back severely into a bun, not a hair out of place, eyed them closely. Tess tried not to fidget under her scrutiny. Finally, after a moment of awkward silence, the older woman broke the stillness in the room.

"Well, Detective Haywood, Deputy Dane. To what do I owe the pleasure of this meeting?"

"We are currently investigating two murders, ma'am. We are trying to determine how the two are connected, and the one thing we have found so far is their enrollment at this school," Denny said, direct and to the point. Tess agreed with his tactics. Mrs. Nora Rodriguez-Bates, with her matching shirt and cardigan, a string of pearls around her neck, did not seem the type to mince words.

"Well, I am sorry, Detective," she began. "You've wasted a trip here, I'm afraid. Our students, past and present, expect a certain degree of privacy. I am not at liberty to hand out any personal information. I'm sure you understand."

"Ma'am, I understand your position. Truly, I do," Denny said, not taking his eyes off of the woman. "But these murders are quite gruesome—horrific even. Here, I have photos if you don't–" he said, opening a file.

"Stop!" the headmistress commanded. "I do not need to see such things, Detective."

Tess quickly glanced at Denny's lap and noticed that the file contained no photos. Nora had fallen for his bluff, rewarding Denny with a scowl.

"We have reason to believe that another one of your past students could be in danger, ma'am," Tess said, playing the good cop. "I'm sure, with your help we can try to save his life." Tess watched as the woman's sour expression slightly softened. Tess pressed on gently. "This boy. Do you recognize him?" She held up her cellphone, showing the photo from the swim meet. She'd casually cropped out the part containing Corey Potter. *No need to drum up questions now,* Tess thought.

The headmistress looked at the photo. Even as she shook her head no, her eyes betrayed her. She knew exactly who he was. Undeterred, Tess continued.

"We need to find him, and fast. His life is in extreme danger. Surely you don't want his death on your conscience."

The woman sighed, looking down at her desk. She was quiet for a moment, as though she were at war with herself. Finally, she looked up at Denny, and then Tess.

"His name is Johnny Carpel," Nora said, looking over at Tess's phone again. "He was one of our more... difficult students."

"What do you mean by 'difficult'? Academically? Socially?" Tess inquired, trying to reign in her excitement. Now they had a name!

"Behaviorally. He was constantly getting into trouble on and off campus," the headmistress said sadly. "By the end of his senior year, he'd already been arrested three times for assault and burglary. His GPA was atrocious. It was a relief when he finally withdrew from classes." She paused, looking over Denny's shoulder, deep in thought. "I know that it is cruel to say, but Johnny Carpel just wasn't Sherman Hills material."

"Do you know where he might be these days?" Denny asked, bringing the woman's mind back to focus. She turned and looked at him.

"I honestly don't know," she said. "Once he left here, he just... disappeared." She suddenly sat up straighter and sighed, "Oh, well, look at the time. I am due for another meeting. I hope you find him," she said, bringing the meeting to an abrupt halt. Buzzing for her secretary to escort them out, she stood and offered her hand to each officer in turn. "If we can be of any further assistance, please contact us."

Nora handed them off to the secretary and swiftly disappeared back into the confines of her office, the door shutting firmly behind her.

"Come this way," the receptionist said as she led them out into the hallway toward the school's entrance. They were silent for a moment, the only noise being the distant murmurs of voices down the halls and the sounds of their footfalls on the recently polished floors. They were almost to the front door when the receptionist abruptly stopped and glanced over her shoulder, as though she were looking for someone.

"Please," she whispered, "follow me." As she slipped into the restroom near the front door, Tess and Denny looked at each other in confusion and then followed her cautiously. After glancing out into the vestibule once more, and then under the stall doors, the receptionist finally stood and looked at them.

"I have to be quick, or they will come looking for me," she whispered, her eyes large.

"Who will?" Denny asked, confused.

"The headmistress. Campus security," the receptionist said, fear on her face. "They don't want anybody talking to you. I overheard them before you got here this morning. I could lose my job right now." She paused, looking at the bathroom door behind Denny nervously.

"What do you know? Do you know anything about Johnny Carpel's current whereabouts?" Denny asked.

"Or anything about this tattoo?" Tess asked, holding up the photo for her to see.

"Yes and no. I don't know where he is today. It's been years. But he and I dated all of junior and senior year. I used to be a student here also," the receptionist said. "He was always causing trouble, and we eventually fell apart. He had just changed too much, and I couldn't do it anymore. As for the tattoo, they all had one."

"They? Who are they?" Denny asked, trying to reign in his excitement at a possible new lead.

"The Phoenix? At least that's what he told me," the receptionist offered. "It was some secret club or something that he and his friends formed senior year."

"Do you know who else was in the club?" Tess asked hopefully.

"I remember Corey Potter and—"

The door to the bathroom swung open just then, a tall wisp of a girl entering. She stopped suddenly at seeing the three adults huddled in the restroom, whispering, and gave them a wide berth. The receptionist tensed and then, making her way to exit quickly, mumbled, "I'm sorry. I've said too much."

Chapter Twenty-Five

Monday, October 31st, 12:04 p.m.

"Ok. Like what just happened in there?" Tess said as she and Denny pulled out of the school's parking lot. The day was gray and overcast as Tess looked out the window.

"Super cryptic," Denny agreed, weaving through traffic. "It's like she was scared of something."

"Other than losing her job, I really don't know what," Tess said, reaching over to turn up the air some. "At least we found the name of the other tattooed boy. We can run the name when we get back to the station. See if there are any hits."

"What kind of club do you think the Phoenix was?" Denny asked, turning onto the interstate toward home. "It's kind of a cheesy name, right?"

"Almost as bad as the tattoos themselves," Tess agreed.

"Who knows. Teenagers are weird," Denny said, making a face. Tess laughed.

"Well, a phoenix is supposed to symbolize rebirth or immortality, right?" she asked. "What if the boys thought they were invincible or untouchable or something—like nobody could stop them?"

Denny seemed to ponder the thought for a moment. "I could see that. You get some arrogant, hormone-driven teenage boys that think they are untouchable and who knows what all they could get into—especially if they were hanging out with the likes of Johnny Carpel. Sounds like he was a troublemaker from the beginning."

"I'm guessing that whatever they got into was bad enough to get our killer fired up, to the point that he decided to go after them. It's the only link we have so far. Both men went to the same school and have the same tattoo. Until proven otherwise, I'd say this case is based on simple, old-fashioned revenge."

Monday, October 31st, 2:45 p.m.

After getting back to the police station, Denny and Tess went to work running Johnny Carpel's name through the criminal database, looking for any hits of past indiscretions. There were quite a few variations of Johnny

Carpel's name. As Denny went to get them some lunch, Tess sat at the computer and scrolled through the different profiles, looking for the correct one.

"That one is too old," she mumbled to herself as she changed search parameters. Assuming Johnny Carpel was a senior in 1998 when Corey Potter was at the school, he would have been born in or around—

"1980," Tess said aloud, counting backwards with her fingers. She typed the year into the search engine, then decided to add 2 years on either side of her search parameters in the chance that he'd been held back in school and was older or younger than they thought. Hitting 'enter', she waited as the computer processed her request. Within moments, five different profiles loaded on her screen. Grabbing her cell phone, she zoomed into the photo of the boy at the pool and began scrolling through the search results.

"That one is too blond and pale," she muttered, clicking to the next one. "That one is the wrong race." She clicked to the next one. "That one is too tattooed. Yikes," she said, making a face at all the facial tattoos and piercings, not to mention the man's cold stare that sent a chill down her spine. She clicked to the fourth one, and there he was: John Evan Carpel. Quickly comparing the boy in the pool picture to that of the slightly older man staring back at her from the computer screen, she knew she'd found her man. As she began scrolling through the file, Denny got back.

"Looks like you found him?" He asked, handing her the Cobb salad she'd ordered. She nodded her thanks and quickly set about opening the dressing packet to apply it to her meal.

"Looks like it, born in November of '79, six foot, three inches tall... phoenix tattoo on chest, along with a rose tat on his right bicep... got picked up in 1999 for assault. Apparently he got into a fight with another teen at a grocery store on Broad Street in Columbus. The fight got out of control, and some food displays were damaged. He spent the night in jail for it, but the other kid's parents apparently asked for a reduced sentence. He ended up with community service and a mandatory anger management class."

"Sounds like a hot head. Anything else?" Denny asked before taking a bite of his turkey club sandwich.

"Just stupid stuff like breaking and entering, jay walking, and possession. He's somehow lucked out every time, only having short jail sentences or community service."

"When was the last offense?"

"Ummm..." Tess said, scrolling through the arrest information. "About ten years ago: a breaking and entering charge back in June of 2013. It looks like he spent four months in jail for those shenanigans. He's basically been in and out of the system until that last time in 2013. Then it's been radio silence."

"It doesn't really make any sense. How did he go from being in and out of jail for most of his twenties and then suddenly nothing?"

"He's not incarcerated. I already checked," Tess said.

"And he's not dead. There is no death certificate listed," Denny said, thinking. "Maybe he moved out of Ohio and is laying low? Or he's out gallivanting the globe somewhere?"

"It does have a last known address, listed just out of Columbus," Tess said. "Want to check it out?"

"Sure. It's probably a long shot given how old the information is. Is there any next of kin or known associates listed?" Denny asked, finishing off his sandwich.

"No known associates," Tess read. "But there is a name for his father: Edward James Carpel. Addresses match."

"I guess we are going back to Columbus."

Chapter Twenty-Six

Monday, October 31st, 6:48 p.m.

The Carpel home was nice. The front porch was freshly painted, the flowerbeds well-managed. A 'Welcome to our Home' sign hung next to the black painted door. Two large pumpkins flanked the door next to a miniature scarecrow and small bales of straw.

As it was almost 7:00 p.m., the sun had already set. It was Halloween night, and the sidewalks were filled with children of all ages going house to house trick-or-treating. Watching the flow of costumes pass by, kids laughing and parents calling for them to slow down, Tess and Denny climbed the steps to the Carpel home. The temperature was dropping and sent a shudder up Tess's spine as they rang the doorbell. A moment or so later, the porch light flipped on, and an older man stood there, holding a bowl of candy.

"Can I help you?" He asked, looking the newcomers over closely. He'd obviously been expecting kids at his door.

"Hello. I am Detective Haywood with the Ohio Bureau of Criminal Investigation," Denny gestured toward Tess. "And this is my partner, Deputy Tess Dane. Are you Edward Carpel?"

The man nodded, a sudden look of suspicion on his face. "Yeah, that's me. What can I do for you?"

"Well, sir, we have some questions about your son, Johnny," Denny said. "Would we be able to speak in private? It's somewhat urgent."

"What's that boy done now?" Edward said, his look of suspicion turning to defeat. He sighed and then moved to the side, opening the front door wider for them. Leading them into the dimly lit living room, he set the candy down on the end table.

"Who's here, Ed? Who are you talking to?" called a woman's voice from upstairs. "Is it Nancy?"

"No, Sharon," Edward called up to her. "It's the police. Here to talk about Johnny."

"Johnny? What's he done now?" Sharon said, as she came down the stairs and into the living room. "Oh. It *is* the cops. You two look like cops," she told Denny as she turned to her husband. "Are they really cops? Did you see their badges?" Edward shook his head.

"Ed!" Sharon reprimanded, drawing his name out with a distinct whine. "You're always supposed to check badge numbers. There are imposter cops out there just waiting to rob you blind."

"Ma'am?" Denny interrupted the woman's tirade. She turned to him abruptly and eyed the badge he was holding in his hand. She harrumphed and then found a seat on the rose-colored couch.

"So, what's this all about?" Edward said, gesturing for the investigators to have a seat before taking one himself.

"Well, sir, we are looking for your son, Johnny," Tess said, taking the lead. "We have reason to believe he could be in some danger."

"Danger?" exclaimed Sharon. "What kind of danger? He hasn't joined the mob or anything, has he?" She stared at Tess through her thick glasses, her eyes large and unblinking.

"Well, ma'am, we are currently investigating a string of murders and have reason to believe your son is at risk," Tess said, trying to keep her voice level.

"He's not my son," Sharon said, as though Tess should already know that.

"Um... ok. But do you know where he is?" Tess asked, somewhat surprised that the woman was more concerned about Tess knowing he wasn't her son than she was that his life may be in danger.

"Nope," Sharon said, sitting back on the couch.

"We haven't seen him in years," Edward said, sadness crossing his round face. He reached up and scratched his balding head, seemingly deep in thought. "He got into a lot of trouble in his early years, especially after senior year—in and out of jail," he paused. "I'm sure you already know that though."

"He was a student at Sherman Hills, correct?" Denny said. The other man nodded.

"Johnny started down the wrong path freshman year. He was amazingly smart and had a bright future. He did very well for himself at the school until his mom died. He was fifteen when she was killed in a car accident," Edward said, looking down at the coffee table for a moment. "They were very close. He took it very badly but started making bad decisions as a way to cope. I never understood it."

"I'm sorry to hear that, Mr. Carpel," Denny said sympathetically. "I also have a child that has lost her mother. It's so hard being the remaining parent and not being able to help them through the mourning process."

Edward nodded, glancing up at Denny before quietly wiping at his eyes. "Why do you think he's in danger now? Is it something to do with drugs?"

"We've had two men murdered in the past week, and both attended Sherman Hills. They also had a phoenix tattoo on their chest," Tess said, watching Edward and Sharon for any sign of reaction. Nothing. And then, Edward sighed.

"He got that ugly thing during senior year. He and his secret club—or whatever the hell it was—all got them. I'm pretty sure they tattooed each other, but I don't know for sure."

"What did he say about the club? Who was in it?" Tess asked, her mind racing.

"Not much. It wasn't a real club or anything. Mostly just him hanging out with some friends from school. They decided to tattoo each other right after graduation. They said they were unstoppable; nothing could touch them. They, in their minds, were going to take over the world," Edward snorted with a shrug.

"They? Do you know the names of the other boys in the group?"

"There were four of them, if I remember correctly. Johnny, Corey Potter, and Greg somebody." Edward said thinking. Then snapped his fingers. "No, it was Gary. Gary Hinsley. That was it."

"And the fourth boy?" Tess gently prodded.

"Quiet fellow. Didn't say much," Edward said, scrunching up his face, thinking. He turned to Sharon. "Do you remember?"

"No, I only saw him once," Sharon offered. "Dark hair... skinny as a rail... I don't know if I ever knew his name."

Tess sighed quietly. They just needed the name of the fourth boy because he could be their killer. And if he wasn't, then maybe he knew who was.

"Do you guys have any idea where Johnny could be now? Last known address?" Denny asked. "According to our records, his driver's license is expired, and there are no outstanding warrants or arrests."

"Sorry, Detective," Edward said, looking defeated. "After he got out of jail the last time, he just... left. He said he needed a change of scenery, and then he walked out. No phone calls, no emails, no visits."

"Something you said a moment ago... that the boys got the tattoos right after graduation?" Tess asked, deep in thought. "The headmistress at Sherman Hills said that Johnny withdrew from class. Is that true? Or did he graduate?"

Edward Carpel sighed. "Officially on paper? Yes, technically he graduated, but just barely. His GPA was hardly passing by that point. He was constantly getting into trouble at school, but then right after senior prom, he was dismissed from classes abruptly and asked not to return to school grounds. There were only like three weeks left of school at that point, and he had to finish his work at home. It was horrible, trying to get him to buckle down and do the work. We got into so many fights. Some even turned physical."

Sharon reached over then and took her husband's hand in hers. "I didn't want to be alone with him during that time. He scared me," she said. "It was like something had happened in his mind, and he thought he was invincible. He began pushing me around, threatening me. Well... not actual threats, but enough of a sinister tone in his voice that I was worried about my safety."

"Any idea why he was suddenly asked not to come back to class?" Denny asked.

"The school didn't say for sure. Just that there had been an issue with Johnny—an incident. But they weren't at liberty to discuss it," Edward said. "I was too afraid to push the issue any further. Johnny was volatile at that time, and the school was unhelpful. All Johnny would tell me was that he was being blamed for something he didn't do. He said that the school and some of the other students were threatening him, so he'd fought back to protect himself. But now, after talking to you guys, I'm beginning to think it was all lies."

Chapter Twenty-Seven

Monday, October 31ˢᵗ, 10:02 p.m.

They rode back to Tess's in silence, each deep in thought. It was late, and Tess was tired. It had been a long Monday. She felt bad about working such long hours and leaving Otter at home alone so much. Maybe he'd like an extra day at doggie daycare this week, she thought. She usually sent him every Wednesday, but it couldn't hurt him to go two days in a row.

"What are you thinking about?" Denny said, pulling her out of her thoughts as he turned down her street to drop her off. "You've been pretty quiet since leaving the Carpels."

"I don't know. I'm just tired," she said, stifling a yawn. "I'm having dog-mom guilt over leaving Otter alone so much. I think I'll take him to daycare tomorrow."

Denny smiled. "He'll like that." He pulled into her driveway and put the car in park. "We have an early morning update meeting with the sheriff. I'll probably be up for a while tonight cyber stalking Johnny Carpel." He sighed, glancing at his watch. "Talk about dog-mom guilt. My kid has been with my neighbor since after school today." He hung his head, then looked back up at Tess's darkened house.

"I'm sorry, Denny. It can't be easy, but you seem to be doing a great job."

"Thanks," he sighed again. "It's really tough. I'm not going to lie. Here we are two years out, and I still feel like I'm failing her." He looked over at Tess, his face in shadow. "I hear her crying at night sometimes—crying for her mom. When I go to console her, she usually wakes up sobbing, then clings to me so tight," he confessed, as his voice broke a little. "I don't know how to make her hurt go away, Tess. I think maybe it is easier for me to work through things because I'm an adult, but Natalie is just a kid."

"I thought you'd taken her to therapy. Maybe just talking about it can help?"

"Yeah, we've tried that. We went together and separately. I got a lot from it," he said. "I think she did too but... I don't know. I think that when you lose someone close to you, there is always an empty spot where they should be. There is always going to be a spot in you that is for them and them alone, even when you move on. But when that person is an actual part of you, like a mother or father, the wound never quite heals."

Tess was quiet for a while, thinking about her own strained relationship with her mother. Natalie's situation was quite different, of course, but Tess felt as though her own mother was already gone as well in some respects. Tess had given up on a relationship with her mother long ago.

"I understand what you mean though. I've lost both of my parents really, even though they are both still alive. One wants nothing to do with me, and the other can't remember me most days. It's hard and even though I've had time to process my reality, it still hurts. I don't think it will ever heal all the way."

"Speaking of your dad," Denny said changing the subject, "How is he? Didn't you say he had some kind of episode the other night?"

"Yeah. Saturday night," Tess said, looking out the windshield at her dark house. A light rain had started and was drumming out a quiet rhythm on the car's roof. "The nurse called late and said he'd flipped out while watching TV and started punching orderlies. Yelling something like 'make them pay!' but I don't even know what it means."

"Watching TV?" Denny questioned, "Sounds like a mob movie or something." He smiled.

Tess laughed lightly. "No, I think Angela said it was the news. But I don't know what would set him off. The meteorologist getting the weather wrong?"

"Maybe he was mad over something political? Or maybe he saw something about the murders, and he wants the killer to pay? You know, once a cop, always a cop."

"Good point," Tess agreed. "Dad has wanted to be in law enforcement since he was a kid. Anyway, whatever got him upset, he was quiet by the time I got there. He was even lucid for a few moments before he got confused again. That was nice—having a few moments with him." She smiled sadly, wishing she got more time like that with her dad.

Just then, Otter must have finally noticed Denny's car parked in the driveway. Tess and Denny could hear his excited barks all the way inside the car.

"You better go," Denny said laughing. "That dog is going to tear your curtains down if you don't."

"True, true," Tess said, gathering her things to exit the vehicle. "See you tomorrow morning." And with a light squeal as the cold October rain fell on her, she ran all the way into the house, waving to Denny before she shut the door.

Chapter
Twenty-Eight

Monday, October 31st, 10:36 p.m.

It was well after ten when Evan Anderson got home from work. A light rain had just started as he put his house key in the lock and opened his door. With a sigh of relief, he was glad to be home. Working at a call center sucked. It was boring and mind numbing, the hours long. But *beggars can't be choosers.*

He'd been working at the call center for a few months now and things seemed to finally be paying off. His past was behind him, and his future looked bright and sunny. He had his own place now, an apartment near Camden Town. *No more roommates for me!* he thought with a smile as he headed into the kitchen, flipping on the light. He went to the fridge to get a drink.

Unscrewing the lid off of the milk jug in the fridge, he threw his keys on the counter before taking a long swig of milk directly from the jug. He could do that now. This was his home, and nobody could tell him he couldn't.

Recapping the milk, he put the jug back into the fridge and rummaged around inside looking for something to eat.

"Hello, Evan," came a voice directly behind him. "Or should I say... Johnny?"

Evan straightened and whirled around to see a man standing in his kitchen.

"What the fuck man?!" Evan shouted, leaning into the opened fridge, the coldness of the interior cooling his suddenly sweaty skin. "Who the fuck are you?"

"Let's just say—I'm your worst nightmare," the man said, taking a step toward him. Evan didn't recognize him. He was young, maybe early twenties, wearing jeans, an old tee shirt, and hiking boots.

Evan started to panic. "What do you want? I don't have anything worth stealing." Then he thought of the coffee can full of cash hidden in his bedroom. "I have some money. If I give it to you, will you just leave?"

"If only it was that easy, *Johnny*," the man said, putting emphasis on his last word. Johnny. How did he know about that? Evan hadn't been called Johnny for over ten years. He'd made sure of it, leaving no trace of his past. Or had he? Somehow, the man standing in his kitchen knew exactly who he was.

As Evan stood there, his mind going a mile a minute, he was distracted—distracted enough that when he finally saw the gun in the man's hand, it was too late.

"Here. Put these on," the man commanded, throwing a pair of handcuffs onto the counter. "And no funny business, or I'll kill you."

Evan tried to steady his shaking hands as he reached out to pick up the handcuffs. He was starting to get the feeling that the man didn't intend to kill him now, but he did intend to kill him. As the thought planted itself in his racing mind, Evan felt his heart reel out of control. Despite his attempts to steady his hands, they shook as he awkwardly put the handcuffs around his wrist. He could feel the man with the gun standing just a few feet away watching his every move.

Once the handcuffs were in place, Evan held his hands up. The man took another step forward, and, still holding the gun in one hand, checked that the cuffs were tight.

Evan looked up from the cuffs then, but as he moved, the stranger swung the butt of the gun into Evan's temple. The man's sneer was the last thing Evan saw as he crumpled to his kitchen floor.

Monday, October 31st, 11:58 p.m.

With a grunt, Brian pulled Johnny's unconscious body from the trunk of his car, dumping him unceremoniously onto the hard forest floor. With a little scoping out beforehand, Brian had determined that this spot, hidden among the trees, would be the best place to hide his car while he finished up with Johnny Carpel. *Johnny fucking Carpel,* Brian thought with an eye roll. It had taken him a little time to track the man down, but then he'd figured out why.

The idiot had taken on his deceased mother's maiden name and changed his first name to his actual middle name making him Evan Anderson. Brian assumed that Johnny was trying to avoid his unsavory past, but the joke was on him. No matter how much he'd changed himself on paper, the sins of his past still haunted Johnny—no, *Evan.* And tonight, he'd pay for his actions.

Brian slammed the trunk of the car, looking around the dark woods for prying eyes, but of course they were alone. He bent down and grabbed Johnny by the ankles, and drug him toward the clearing. Slinging Johnny's limp body over a felled tree, Brian began tying his prey's feet and arms in such a way that no matter how hard Johnny fought, he'd never get loose. Setting up a battery-operated camp lantern near Johnny, Brian set about getting his tools ready.

Johnny let out a slight moan as he began regaining consciousness.

"Oh good, you're waking up," Brian said, grabbing a handful of Johnny's hair and pulling his head up to look at his face. A large bruise was already forming over Johnny's left eye from where Brian had hit him. Brian smiled.

"Fuck you, man," Johnny said, suddenly coming to enough to realize he was bound and couldn't move. "You got the wrong man."

"Oh, I assure you I don't, Johnny," Brian said, letting go of Johnny's hair and watching his head flop forward, nearly hitting the rough bark of the tree.

"Why do you keep calling me that?" Johnny asked, panic in his voice. "My name is Evan Anderson."

"You might go by Evan Anderson now, but you were born John Evan Carpel. Don't try to deny it. I did my homework. You thought you'd be sneaky and just use your mom's maiden name of Anderson like nobody would notice," Brian stated as he made his way around Johnny. "Boy, were you wrong. Just a little digging, and I had everything I needed to know. The internet is a wonderful thing, don't you think?"

Johnny's mouth went dry, his breathing coming in shallow gasps. He didn't deny it. When he remained silent, Brian grinned to himself.

"Your silence is enough for me, so let's cut the shit," Brian said, walking back around to face Johnny—this time with something in his hands. Johnny gulped when he realized it was an axe. "Do you know why I brought you here? Have you figured it out yet?"

"I don't know man. Did I rob your house or something?" Johnny said, a look of desperation etched into his anguished face.

"Let me give you a hint, since you obviously don't remember," Brian snapped, anger spreading to his features. He shined a flashlight in Johnny's face while the axe dangled from the other hand. Johnny squinted against the sudden illumination in his eyes.

"Does the name Maggie Sloane ring any bells?" Brian asked, still shining the light in his prey's face. He grinned ominously as he watched the color drain from Johnny's face.

"Ahhhh... so you *do* know why we are out here then," Brian said smugly. "Tsk Tsk, Johnny. Best not to lie to me! I know who you really are. I know all the shit you've done. And worst of all, I know that you never paid for your sins, now did you?"

Johnny's eyes went wide, and he started flailing, pulling against his restraints. When he realized his efforts were futile, he began screaming. Brian angrily dropped the axe with a thud and pulled a bandana from his back pocket. Using it to gag Johnny's mouth to silence him, he leaned down to whisper in Johnny's ear. "You've had nearly thirty years of freedom, but tonight, you will pay for your sins, with interest."

This caused Johnny to flail even more, his muffled cries and pleads falling on deaf ears. He watched then as Brian picked up the axe, spinning it slightly in his hands, the lantern light glinting off of the sharpened blade. Brian, a sinister grin on his face, slowly made his way behind Johnny once more.

"Did you really think you'd get away with it? That no one would ever know?" Brian spat. "You ruined her life. You ruined my life. You just went about your own business la-de-da like you hadn't destroyed someone."

Johnny began sobbing in earnest, and then Brian noticed a darkening stain on the seat of Johnny's pants.

"Did you just piss yourself? God, you're pathetic," Brian sneered. "You can't even face your own reality without pissing yourself like a fucking toddler!"

Johnny's sobs only increased, angering Brian even further.

"You went around acting like you were 'Mr. Tough Guy' after you totally shattered someone, and now you can't even control your bladder. You're disgusting. I can't stand here all night listening to you sniffle. You want something to cry about? Huh? Let me give you something to cry about as you think about how worthless you really are. Have you ever heard of a Blood Eagle?"

As Johnny's muffled wails filled the dark, silent woods, the axe came down onto his back, the blade ripping into his flesh.

Chapter Twenty-Nine

Tuesday, November 1st, 11:15 a.m.

"So, you think you're gonna make it with Molly next weekend?" Dylan Cramer asked as he and his two best friends, Sam and Blake, slowly made their way through the tangle of undergrowth. The trio of highschoolers were playing hookie (again) and had decided to explore the back acreage of Yardley Game Reserve, just outside of Camden Town. The area was popular for hikers, backpackers, and bored teenagers such as themselves.

"What makes you think I haven't already?" Blake said with a smug smile. Sam snorted.

"Please. If you tapped that, you *woulda* told us," Dylan said, laughing. "I bet you haven't even felt her up yet."

"Have you even kissed her?" Sam asked, his face full of amusement. Blake stopped walking and just gave Sam and Dylan a look. With a huff, he set off down the trail again.

"You guys are losers," he called back over his shoulder. "Of course we've kissed. I just don't kiss and tell." He grinned to himself.

"Whatever you say, Blake," Sam said, rolling his eyes, as they continued walking down the narrow, overgrown animal trail. The boys had been there multiple times in the past, and with each trip the trail seemed to widen ever so much. They were headed to their usual hangout. Just a random, isolated clearing in the woods that they'd made their own.

Sam and Dylan looked at each other and grinned. They thoroughly enjoyed picking on Blake and his conquests—or lack thereof—with his new girlfriend, Molly Reed. Everybody at Camden High knew Molly was basically married to Jesus and would never stray down such an immoral path of impurity before she was married. Both Sam and Dylan knew there was next to zero chance of Molly caving to somebody like Blake, and they reminded him of such almost daily.

Up ahead of them, Blake was walking with his head down, looking at his phone.

"Is Molly texting?" Sam called. "Did she send you a pic of her boobs?" This sent Dylan and Sam into a fit of laughter.

"You two are so immature," Blake said, rolling his eyes and ignoring them. He looked around the forest surrounding him. Dappled light from the afternoon sun played peekaboo with the shadows of the undergrowth. Though many leaves had already turned color and fallen to the forest floor, enough were still on the trees, igniting the canopy in an array of oranges and reds. Blake sighed deeply, the earthy damp scent of molding leaves and mud filling his nostrils. He loved this time of year best of all. The days were getting cooler, and it would be Thanksgiving soon. He was planning on inviting Molly to the Culversons' annual Friendsgiving, as they liked to call it.

As he walked ahead of the other boys, he thought about how he'd like to ask her to the party. What if she thought that it sounded lame? He sighed. He knew he was overthinking it as always. He wanted things to go smoothly with Molly. Even though she was super into church and choir, she was very sweet. He liked her a lot, not that he'd tell his friends. They'd just make rude comments and gestures again, and he hated it when they said stuff about Molly.

The wind picked up then, churning leaves around the boys' ankles in little cyclones. Blake was zipping the rest of his hoodie up when a smell assaulted his nostrils. The wind came again, the smell worsening.

"What is that smell?" Blake said, holding his arm up over his nose. He cast a glance around him but saw nothing except his friends stopped on the trail behind him.

The other two boys stood motionless on the trail, side by side, with their shirts pulled up over their noses as the fetid smell continued to waft toward them from the direction of the clearing.

"Maybe it's Dylan's feet?" Sam teased.

"Maybe it's your mom's pussy?" Dylan commented back causing Sam to laugh. Blake just shook his head in disdain and then continued on down the path.

He was some distance away from the other two, their murmuring voices carrying with the wind. As he approached the clearing, it was as though the scent of rot and death became stronger. Blake made a face. A deer better not have died in their clearing. What a mess that would make.

Leaving the other two boys behind him he pressed onward to the clearing, and as he rounded the large live oak at its entrance, he came to a skidding halt. The sight before him was so hideous, so depraved that he started to feel faint, his breath coming out in shallow puffs. As he turned to run away, his toe caught a tree root and sent him flying. He landed with a thud, knees scraping hard on the ground as the air escaped his chest. Blake heard the sound of heaving panting, something taking in wheezing, ragged breaths. And then he realized it was himself. What was that in the clearing? That creature, bloodied and mutilated, hanging from the tree? *Run!* His mind screamed at him as he fumbled his way to his feet. He took off running, nearly colliding with Sam and Dylan, as he escaped the clearing in the woods—and the dead man left there to rot.

Chapter Thirty

Tuesday, November 1st, 12:02 p.m.

"Lights and sirens, boys!" Denny called into the radio as he pressed the accelerator even farther. Tess held her usual spot on the dashboard, silently disheartened that they were yet again headed to a crime scene. By the sounds of dispatch and the first responder, this scene was quite possibly the worst the county, the state, had ever seen.

There was a trail of police vehicles behind them as they sped down the rural road to Yardley Game Reserve. At least this time they should have a few hours of sunlight left to process the scene.

As they approached the turn off, Denny slowed the Tahoe to make the turn. Ahead of them sat a police cruiser with three young boys leaning up against it, their faces ashen. The police officer standing with them motioned for Denny to go on by to park farther down the trail. Denny followed directions and came to a halt a few feet from a small trail leading into the woods. Another officer stood at the trailhead and waited for them to approach.

"Detective," Officer Bailey greeted them. "We need to stop meeting like this."

"Agree," Denny said with a nod. "What do we have?"

"Let's just say… Corey Potter and the Breaking Wheel makes this look like child's play." Officer Bailey motioned for Tess and Denny to follow him down the narrow path through the woods. Shouldering her camera case, Tess looked around her and took in the beautiful scenery. She knew what she was about to see would haunt her dreams until she died.

"Oops, watch your step there," Bailey said, sidestepping a large root across the path.

"I'm guessing those kids back there found it?" Denny asked as they all walked along the uneven ground. Tess, bringing up the rear, sped up so she could hear Officer Bailey.

"Yes, the one did. According to the two other boys, the one came out of the clearing back here, screaming and hysterical. With his reaction and the overpowering stench of decomp, they all just ran out and called us. The first boy is still shaking and can't talk without sobbing. I honestly have no idea what to expect," Bailey said as they approached the scene. "I only got here myself just moments before you guys."

They approached the clearing, the rancid odor of death getting stronger with each step. Tess noticed that Bailey hung back a bit before following her and Denny around the massive oak tree and into the clearing. It was then that they all took a collective intake of breath and stared at the scene before them.

There, suspended from a large tree across the small clearing, hung a man. What was left of him anyway. His arms and legs were each tied taut with rope, causing him to splay out from the branches like Da Vinci's Vitruvian Man. Although he was naked and bloodied, there appeared to be something strange on his back. Almost as though he had wings of some kind.

It was then that Tess knew what she was looking at, what the wings truly were. She felt bile rising in her throat. She barely made it to the edge of the clearing before vomiting up the contents of her stomach. As she started to dry-heave, she let out a sob. She felt Denny come over and place a hand on her back in comfort. She wiped her mouth and then stood, shaking, trying to regain control of her emotions once again.

"It's a Blood Eagle," she said miserably, the words heavy on her tongue.

"A what?" Bailey asked, unable to take his eyes off of the hideous display in front of him.

"A Blood Eagle," Tess repeated.

"Shit," Denny said, awareness dawning on him, "like on that Vikings show?" Tess nodded in response.

"What Viking show? What's a Blood Eagle?" Bailey asked, finally looking at Tess and then Denny.

"A Blood Eagle was allegedly a Viking ceremony or ritual that involved torture and death. They basically would cut the victims ribs off of the spine with an axe or knife and then pull the rib cage open from behind. The rib cage then looks like wings. If that wasn't bad enough, they'd then pull the lungs out through the holes they made. The person would end up dying from suffocation and blood loss," Tess said, reciting what she'd researched.

"That can't be true. That's too much," Bailey said, a look of disbelieving horror on his face. "It's disgusting."

"There are some sources that say it was just a myth. Others say that it really happened. Who knows for sure," Tess said as she slowly started skirting the crime scene and snapping pictures. "Some even say that it was believed that if you didn't make a sound as the Blood Eagle was being performed on you, when you were dead you'd go to Valhalla."

"Wow. That's horrible. Where do you get this stuff from?" Denny said, following behind her. Bailey stayed rooted to the ground near the large live oak.

"Well, when our guy started going after people and torturing them, I *kinda* went down a rabbit hole of torture and totally messed up ways to kill people," Tess said, her face hard. They'd made their way around the dead man in the tree and as they stood there viewing him from this angle, Tess's stomach roiled again.

It was just as she'd expected. The man's ribs had been hacked away from his spine and then pulled open, like flaps on a cardboard box. The racks of ribs reminded her too much of baby back ribs, and she knew then she'd never eat barbecue again.

Pulled out from the holes in the man's thoracic cavity were the lung lobes, crusted with dried blood. The sound of flies buzzing was intense as they set about doing their work on the flesh. Maggots wriggled about in the soupy mixture of blood and body fluids.

"You ever notice how a wave of maggots kind of sounds like a bowl of Rice Krispies cereal when you pour milk on it?" Denny asked, as he stepped over the wriggling white larvae that had fallen from the body and into a puddle of human liquids on the ground at his feet. Tess turned and gave him a look. He just shrugged and continued to follow her.

They circled around to the front of the man and took in the scene. The man's face, battered and bloodied, lulled to the right, his chin resting on his chest. There were multiple small slices in his flesh, mostly on his arms and chest. Farther down, it was obvious that he'd also been emasculated.

"I'm thinking our theory is somehow true," Denny said, looking at the man's pelvis. "We've got three men now, all tortured, all emasculated. Two confirmed to have gone to Sherman Hills Prep School and who also had the same tattoo. I'm guessing we get this guy back to the lab, get him cleaned up and ID'd, that we'll find that he went to the same school and has the same tattoo."

"They've all been emasculated, and these killings are extremely violent. Way over the top," Tess thought aloud. She took a few more steps ahead of Denny when her eye caught something in the undergrowth near the crime scene.

"What's that?" she asked, pointing to the object. Denny approached the underbrush and smiled.

"It looks like a wallet. And back farther is a pair of men's pants," he said, looking around him for more discarded articles. Tess came up beside him and looked over his shoulder as he crouched next to the wallet. She took some photographs and then Denny very carefully opened the wallet, using an ink pen so he didn't touch it. They were in luck. An Ohio driver's license stuck out from behind a credit card and Denny pulled on a glove before carefully pulling it out and reading the name.

"Evan Anderson," Denny read. "It looks like he lived just outside of Columbus. That means, somebody either lured him here, or he was brought against his will."

"This must be the fourth boy in the 'club'," Tess said, thinking aloud. "Gary, Corey, Johnny, and Evan." She leaned in to see the driver's license better and gasped. "Denny! I don't know what's going on here, but doesn't that picture of Evan look a lot like an older version of Johnny Carpel?" She pulled out her phone to find the photo of Johnny at the swim meet and compared it to the picture on the license. It looked to be the same person.

Turning her phone so that Denny could see, she asked, "Isn't this crazy?"

"Not crazy," Denny said. "Incredible, but not crazy. I think you're on the right track though. Now we just have to figure out if and what happened, when it happened, and why no charges were brought way back then."

"And where the name 'Evan Anderson' came from. We'll have to run the dead guy's prints and see if they are a match for Carpel," Tess said, glancing up at what remained of the man's brutalized face. "If he really is Johnny, then we still don't know who the fourth boy was. He could be next."

"Or he could be the killer," Denny stated, staring grimly at the driver's license.

Chapter Thirty-One

Tuesday, November 1st, 1:30 p.m.

Brian knew the police scanner he'd bought at the pawn shop was a good purchase. He sat, perched on a barstool at his kitchen counter, fiddling with buttons and knobs until he tuned it to the right channel. *Woohoo! Sounds like they found Johnny!* Brian grinned to himself. *Fucking Johnny: ringleader of the bunch.* He was the one that started everything, the one that deserved the worst death. But Brian had made sure of that.

He leaned back on the barstool, looking around at the small apartment he and his mother had called home for so long. Even though she was rarely home toward the end of her life, the place still felt empty without her. Even now, he could almost conjure up good memories of her dancing with him in the living room or playing hide and seek throughout their own little slice of the world. Even after things began to change and the darkness began clawing at her mind, taking her farther and farther away from him, he still loved her. Even when she'd used what grocery money they did have on drugs, smokes, booze... he still loved her. Even through all the men traipsing through their house at all hours of the night, even through all the nasty words and physical violence he'd endured, he still loved her.

"I got them, Mama," he whispered. "All except the last one. But don't worry. I'll get him for you." He sighed. The sound of the ticking clock in the living room lulled him deeper into his dark thoughts.

Today was the day, he thought. Today he ended this.

Tuesday, November 1st, 4:51 p.m.

"Hey, Dane, I have a package for you," Ricky Osbourne said, sticking his head into the conference room where Tess and Denny were discussing logistics for the next course of action. They were waiting for the sheriff to finish up a phone call in the next room. It was almost dinner time, and Tess had been thinking about food until Ricky showed up.

"Osbourne, she doesn't want your package. She's already told you no like ten times," Denny said, giving the patrol deputy a scowl.

"Har har, Detective," Osbourne said, scrunching his face up. "I'm talking about this package, but whatever." He handed a padded manila envelope to Tess as she came around the table for it. As she reached for it, she felt Osbourne's eyes on her. She glared up at his face, tired of avoiding him in an effort to be kind. She was done being kind to everyone, especially when they weren't always kind to her. It was exhausting and she was over it. She'd tried being professional with Ricky also, but he didn't seem to get it.

"Thank you, Deputy Osbourne," she said, cringing inwardly when his fingers touched hers, and he waited a moment too long before letting go.

"Hope you enjoy it," he said with a wink before strutting off down the hallway, whistling a Patsy Cline tune. "See you guys later," he called out before disappearing around the corner.

"Can't anything be done about that?" Tess grumped at Denny. "I am sick and tired of his crap. He's like my dad's age—like, grow up."

Denny smirked, "I told you to just haul off and punch him." At Tess's scowl, he quickly added, "Or just file a complaint with internal affairs?"

"I have, but all they do is talk to him. He'll do better for a while and then he's right back to being a jerk."

"Keep making reports until they listen?" Denny suggested.

Tess just grunted as she looked at the envelope in her hand. It was addressed to her at the station, the returned address blurred.

"What is it?" Denny asked, coming close to look, "or better question: who's it from?"

"I don't know. The returned address is blurred from water or something. Jones? No, James. Brian James something," she read as she opened the envelope and peered inside. It was a book of some kind. She paused before reaching in to pull out the contents—a small, worn blue diary. Sticking out of the top of the diary was a Post-it note. Tess could see something written on it.

"Maybe I should put some gloves on. This is kind of cryptic," she said, turning the package over and trying not to touch it any more than she already had. She stood there, holding it while Denny went to get her some gloves.

Moments later, he came back into the room with the gloves and held one while Tess slipped her hand in. After carefully sliding the other one on, she pulled out the diary and opened it to the sticky note. The message, scrawled in pencil read,

Deputy Dane,

I hope this helps you find the truth. I'm tired of all the lies and secrets. Tell your father thanks for all he did. You are just as good of a cop as he was.

See you soon,

Brian James Sloane

Tess's hands began to tremble as she read the note aloud. Was it really from the killer, the madman that had tortured so many people?

"What did my father have to do with any of this?" she asked, setting the note aside and opening the diary. She flipped through the pages filled with doodles and various entries written in a rainbow assortment of gel pens. Scribbled inside the front cover, it read, *"Diary of Maggie Sloane"* and *"Sophomore year! Finally!"*

"It's the diary of Maggie Sloane, from her sophomore year of high school," Tess said, reading through a random entry. She read aloud, "November 17th, 1997: I went to the mall with Maddie. It was lame so we didn't stay long. Ended up at McDonalds on the way home to get milkshakes. Ran into Corey Potter with his overly white teeth and perfectly flipped hair. He was there with Rose Wilcox, and he wouldn't keep his hands off of her. I swear his hand was even up her skirt at one point. Some people have no class."

"Sounds like she wasn't a real fan of Corey's," Denny said as he sat down at the conference table. Tess carefully sat down, trying not to smudge anything in the diary. "What else does it say?"

Tess flipped through a few pages, looking for more entries involving the names of their victims. Who was Maggie Sloane, and how was she connected to this?

A few pages later, another name stood out: Johnny Carpel. The entry was five short words. "Johnny Carpel is an ass," Tess read aloud. She glanced up and saw Denny writing something down. "Wonder what he did?" she asked him.

"I have no idea, but I do know that the killer wanted us to find something in this book—some truth," Denny said.

"Well, the writer's name is Maggie Sloane, and the package is from a Brian Sloane. Maybe Brian is Maggie's brother or father?" Denny said, a thoughtful look on his face. "I'll check them all out. I want this thing over with." As he left the room to run Brian's name through the database, Tess turned back to the book in her hand.

She began flipping through the diary, skimming pages as she went. Entries about mundane things like movies, gossip, daydreams, and shopping filled the pages—typical teenage girl stuff.

A few hours into reading the lengthy diary, Tess got to the last few pages when she saw a name she wasn't expecting. Her heart began to race as she quickly read the entry, nausea coursing through her. Now she knew how she was connected to all of the crimes.

Chapter Thirty-Two

June 29, 1998

This is going to be my last entry. I can't do this anymore... keep all this pain inside of me, crushing me. I haven't said a word about this to anyone, but I'm going to write it here for safe keeping. This is the truth, even though I can't utter the words out loud. I am broken beyond repair.

It happened about a month or so ago, the Thursday before prom. Maddie was having a party at her house because her parents were in Cabo. She and her brother, Lucas, had the house to themselves. Maddie was all excited because some of Lucas's friends, a few whom I'd met before, from Sherman Hills were going to be there. I wasn't excited about that. I was kind of more worried about going, if I'm honest. I'd just gotten off a grounding the week before for coming home after curfew and then smarting off to Mom about it. I didn't need any more reasons for her to ground me again. If I went to the party, I'd have to sneak out again. Mom would never let me go if I asked. Anyway, against my better judgment, I went to Maddie's that night. I wish now that I knew what was going to happen. I never would have gone... never in a million years.

The party was going great, people dancing, talking, drinking. Lucas had been able to get some beer and stuff from a coworker at the pizza shop in Crawley, so everyone seemed happy. I had a few sips of beer at first. It tasted like pee and kinda looked like it too. Everyone else seemed to like it. Either that or they were like total liars. I just wanted to fit in, so I choked down some more and before I knew it, I was feeling pretty good.

Chad and Karl had started up a game of Truth or Dare in the living room. The music was blaring, making it hard to hear the "truths", but the "dares" were fun to watch. At one point, Jennifer Holmes had her shirt off and was slinking around in a red push-up bra dancing. I was glad then that I had decided to be a spectator.

After a while of watching them all play the game and drinking, I decided to go to the kitchen to get another beer and some chips. As I rounded the corner, I ran smack into Johnny Carpel and caused his beer to spill all over the floor and down the front of my shirt. I gasped at the coldness and then looked up at his face.

"I'm so sorry," I said. "I wasn't watching where I was going." I grabbed a paper towel from the counter and began dabbing at my shirt and wiping the floor clean. Johnny just stood there, swaying a little on his feet, watching me.

"It's all good," he said. "Shit happens." He turned then and walked around me out toward the living room. I finished wiping up the floor and then looked down at my shirt again. It was still so wet. I decided to find Maddie and ask to borrow a shirt. I found her in the dining room with her tongue down Steve Newhart's throat and decided to just go raid her closet. She was my best friend, and I knew she wouldn't care.

I walked up the stairs, weaving around couples making out, people talking, and headed for Maddie's room. The door was shut so I knocked first and then opened it. No one was inside. I stepped inside her room, closing the door behind me. I quickly rummaged around in Maddie's drawer and found a dry shirt to wear. As I pulled my wet shirt over my head, I saw movement behind me in the mirror. I turned around quickly and found Johnny standing behind me. Grabbing the dry shirt to cover my chest, I backed up away from him.

"You can't be in here," I said, cursing myself for not locking the door, something I will always regret.

"You can't be either then," he said quietly, looking me up and down. I felt naked and exposed even though I was still wearing my jeans and bra. I didn't like the way he kept *staring at me, like I was a piece of meat, and he was a hungry tiger. My breath came quicker, my heart racing.*

"I'm just getting a shirt," I stammered, "You need to leave."

He just stood there, watching me, his pupils large. "Here, let me help you," he said, taking a step toward me. I quickly retreated until my back side made contact with the dresser. Just as he reached for me, I dodged away, headed for the door. But as I turned the knob, I felt it turn on its own. Confused, I pulled it open only to see three more boys standing in the hallway with grins on their faces.

"Hello, Magpie," Corey Potter said. He grinned over his shoulder, and the other two followed him inside the bedroom and closed the door behind them. The music from the living room grew quiet again, the beat still pulsing through the floorboards. It was no match for the hammering of my heart. RUN! My mind screamed. But as I tried to get around the boys and out the door, I felt a hand clamp around my arm. I whipped around, tugging to free myself, panic rising like the rolling bubbles in a boiling pot.

Johnny pulled me to him and before I could even scream, I felt his lips on mine, greedy and rough. I tried to turn my head away, but his grip only tightened as his other arm came around me and pressed me to him. I could feel his body harden against mine and bile stung my throat. As I pushed back at him, I heard the voices of the other boys from somewhere behind me, egging Johnny along and hooting. At some point his hand came up and slid under my bra, squeezing me as his tongue assaulted my mouth. I tried biting him then, tried to get away, but that just seemed to excite them further.

"Take her Johnny!" they chanted, laughing drunkenly. "Show her what it's like!" I struggled and sobbed, snot pouring out of my nose, my mascara leaving dark trails down my tear-laden face. I had to get away.

He grabbed me around the waist again and then threw me back on Maddie's bed. I immediately tried to roll away, to run, but he pushed me back down. I heard the other boys say, "Hold her arms and legs!" I tried screaming again but a hand was clamped down over my face. I felt someone pulling the zipper down on my jeans, felt them being pulled down, followed by my underwear. By this point I was sobbing so hard I could hardly breathe, strong hands holding me down. I knew what was going to happen. Even though the hand was still over my mouth, I screamed, "No!"

My attempts at screaming for help and of fighting back, did nothing to save me. I watched in horror as Johnny Carpel lowered the fly on his jeans while laughing with his friends. As he leaned over me, his nakedness touching me, he whispered in my ear, "I've seen the way you watch me.

I've been watching you, too. I know you want this." And with that, he took my innocence.

I'm not sure how long I laid there, after they each took their turn, bleeding and crying. All I remember was that Corey Potter, Gary Hinsley, Johnny Carpel and Ricky Osbourne all needed to pay. I remember laying there, on the disheveled bed, crying and alone for what seemed like forever. Eventually, Lucas's friend, Tommy Dane, came into the room. He was instantly rushing to me, covering me, helping me up, asking who did it. I tried to tell him what had happened, but he could figure that out just by the sight of me.

He called the cops and came with me to the hospital, Maddie by his side. He eventually told me that he'd seen the boys leaving the bedroom, laughing and joking with each other. He even talked to them for a while on the landing as they were heading downstairs. It was after Corey made some comment about having some fun upstairs that Tommy came to see what had happened. He'd tried to tell the police what had happened. They took down his statement and then, when I was able, they took mine. The cops told us they would look into it. The nurse took evidence off of me, out of me.

But, as I would find out a couple of weeks later, no charges were going to be filed. There was no record of the police reports, and when my parent's lawyers asked to see the evidence, the DNA swabs and samples had mysteriously gone missing. They had swept the whole thing under the rug. Although I have no proof, I believe everything disappeared because Corey's dad is the mayor. They just made it all go away. Gary would have missed out on his football scholarship to OSU, and Corey would never get to pursue a political career like his dad did.

I'm just me, Maggie Sloane. I have no voice. I've been to hell, and I don't know if I will ever come back. No one, other than my parents, and of course, Tommy Dane, knows the truth. He was always kind to me before it happened. Afterwards, he became a close friend. If only he'd come up the stairs just a few minutes earlier.

All of this happened six weeks ago. I will always be changed, my innocence stolen, but I have to remain strong—because I will be a mother soon. I just got the pregnancy result on the stick moments before I decided to write this. Some people would say that I should get rid of the baby, but I don't think I can. Though conceived in violence, I vow now to raise this baby with love. I just hope I can keep that promise.

Chapter Thirty-Three

Tuesday, November 1st, 8:28 p.m.

"Holy shit," Denny muttered, reading the diary. He looked distressed as he ran his fingers through his hair. "There are so many things to unpack here." He turned to Tess, "Brian has to be Maggie's baby, all grown up. Your name was at the first scene because he wanted you on this case. Exactly why? That part I'm not entirely sure of yet."

"And what about the other boy? The one that is still alive. Did you catch that?" Tess said, staring down at the opened pages. "Ricky Osbourne."

"Our Ricky Osbourne, the slimeball?" Denny asked, anger clouding his face. "Once an asshole, always an asshole."

"We have to find Osbourne before it's too late—and Brian Sloane," Tess said gravely. She got up then and went to the phone in the room to call Bertie, the receptionist.

"Bertie, this is Tess Dane. You have Osbourne out on patrol tonight?" she said into the receiver. After a few seconds, "No? Okay. What's his address again?" A pause. "Ok, yeah."

"Let's go find a slimeball," she said, grabbing her jacket. She put the diary carefully back in the manilla folder and took it with her. As she and Denny ran to their car, Tess tried calling Ricky at the number Bertie had supplied.

"He's not answering his phone," Tess said, hitting redial for the third time. She let out a sigh of frustration as the phone yet again went to voicemail. This time she decided to leave a message. "Hey Osbourne, it's Tess. Can you call me when you get this? It's important." She left her number and then disconnected the call, dropping her phone into the center console. She glanced at Denny, and his steel glaze locked with hers. Hopefully they weren't too late.

Twenty minutes later they pulled into the driveway of Osbourne's small white bungalow located near the edge of town.

Tess followed Denny around the car parked in the driveway, Osbourne's old T-Bird, and headed up the uneven stairs to a sagging front porch. Denny knocked on the door but got no response. He knocked harder, the sound echoing through the house… still no response.

"Let's go around back and check. I don't like this," he said, turning to leave. But as they got to the edge of the porch, the sound of breaking glass came from somewhere inside the house, followed by a thud.

"We're going in." Denny said, pulling his firearm. Tess followed suit. As Denny approached the door, he yelled, "Police! Open up!" After a few seconds, he kicked the door down. The door swung inward, bouncing on its hinges. Gun in hand, Denny cautiously entered the house, cast his gaze in every corner of the first room. "Clear," he said, as he went deeper inside. Tess, gun at the ready, followed him into the darkened interior.

The house was dimly lit, the thick curtains drawn tight. Tess could make out the shapes of a couch and chairs to her right and saw an ascending staircase to her left. Piles of old newspapers and magazines lay in stacks scattered around the living room, and the coffee table was covered in old takeout boxes.

Ahead of her, Denny entered the kitchen cautiously, but it was empty. Denny and Tess broke apart to search the lower floor. Denny headed toward the back of the house while Tess made her way slowly down a hallway off the living room. There were three doors along the corridor, two of which were closed. The first was a closet, crammed full haphazardly. The second room was open and turned out to be a bathroom, the fixtures and decor at least two decades old.

Tess couldn't hear or see Denny, and suddenly she felt so alone. She slowly made her way down the carpeted hallway to the last door. She couldn't hear anything from behind the closed door as she came to a stop next to it. Her breathing was coming quickly, and she tried to calm herself. Had Brian already made it here and taken Ricky to torture? Or were they in the house somewhere?

As she approached the door, reaching out silently to grab the doorknob to open it, she heard a noise—a bump—coming from behind it. She swallowed, beads of sweat dotting her forehead. She looked down at the pale light coming from under the door. Suddenly something moved behind it, its shadow moving across the strip of light underneath. Tess jumped back slightly, focusing herself. Reaching her hand out, she slowly grasped the brass knob and turned.

All of a sudden, as she pushed the door inward, a feral growl assaulted her ears followed by a hiss. Tess jumped as a fat black cat came running from the room. As the cat disappeared down the hall, Tess entered the room, only to find it empty. She gave a small sigh of relief as she lowered her weapon, yet still held it at the ready making her way back down the hall. It was then that she noticed a door under the stairs. Curious, she moved over to it and cautiously opened it. Inside, a narrow stairway descended into murky shadows. Tess reached out, feeling for a light switch but felt nothing.

She quickly glanced over her shoulder, looking for Denny but he was nowhere to be seen. She was about to close the basement door and go find him when she heard a muffled sound coming from the shadowy depths in front of her. She strained, trying to hear anything else but was met with silence. Tess stood there for a moment, at the top of the stairs, inwardly wrestling with herself about whether she should wait for Denny or go down and investigate. She had just decided to wait for Denny when she heard another sound—a scraping sound followed by a small, muffled sob. Did Brian have Ricky in the basement, tied up somewhere? Or did Ricky think they knew about his past sins and were there to arrest him?

Another muffled cry floated up from the darkened stairwell, and against her better judgment, Tess began her descent. Annoyed with herself for leaving her cell phone in the car, Tess activated the flashlight app on her smartwatch, wishing she had something more substantial to see by. The thin beam of light barely seemed to illuminate the stairwell as she slowly made her way downward, one step at a time. The sound of her own breathing, anxious and quick, matched the rhythm of her heart. She silently wished she'd waited on Denny. She was about to turn around when she felt something soft brush against her dark hair. Her body instinctively jerked away from the object.

Tess quickly shone the light above her and let out a sigh of relief when she discovered the thin, cotton pull string for the light over her head. It was still moving from where she'd run into it in the darkness. She reached up and pulled it, but nothing happened. It was then that she noticed the light bulb was missing. She let out a small sigh of frustration as she continued on down the long narrow flight of stairs. Watch flashlight aimed ahead of her down the stairs, she took each step cautiously to avoid a fall. The old stairs, wooden and bowing, creaked under her weight.

When her feet were finally on the solid cement floor at the bottom of the staircase, Tess turned around slowly, shining the light around her. Old boxes, stacked in dusty piles, lined the wall in front of her. In the distance, she could hear the dripping of an old pipe. Past the boxes, on the other side of the basement, Tess could see an old hot water tank and more spiderwebs than she cared to think about.

The damp, earthy smell of the room filled her nostrils as she started to move slowly around the area, checking dark corners and behind boxes. Noticing a small glow of flickering light, perhaps from a candle, she slowly made her way through the darkness. She was halfway to the light when she suddenly heard something move behind her. The air seemed to tingle with energy and as she whirled around, something hit the side of her head. She saw stars as she fell to a heap on the cool concrete.

Chapter Thirty-Four

Slowly the darkness receded, but the headache remained. Tess rolled over with a groan, her head pounding. She tried to sit up but felt weak. Something warm ran down her face slowly. Reaching up with her hand, she pulled her fingers back, sticky and wet. Blood.

She slowly sat up and began looking around in the darkness. Her watch was gone. Darkness surrounded her except for the small light seeping from around the stacked boxes in front of her. Her head still throbbed, disorienting her. Where was she? Was she still in the basement? Where was Denny?

Tess climbed onto her hands and knees, bracing herself to stand. Stumbling slightly, her head feeling woozy, she slowly made her way to her feet. She had no idea how long she'd been out, but one thing was for sure. Someone was in the room with her. She could hear them breathing. She turned her head toward the sounds, unable to see much in the limited light.

Pivoting slowly, Tess tried to see anything—some more light or even an object—to orient herself. The blackness surrounding her was as though she had been cast into a dark sea during a storm. Her blood seemed to throb and slosh like waves in her head. Reaching out a tentative hand, she felt nothing but empty air in front of her. Slowly, she took a shuffling step forward, and then another, her hands extended in front of her. If she could just find the stairway, she could make it out of the basement. With that goal at hand, she slowly moved ahead, shuffling her feet and waving her arms around in front of her, trying desperately to find something to anchor herself to.

She felt a slight breeze on her face, and she recoiled instantly. The sound of someone breathing got even closer to her, and she felt the hair on the back of her neck stand at attention. Then it dawned on her. It wasn't a breeze hitting her in the face. It was someone's breath. As she filled her own lungs to scream, a strong hand came from the darkness and clamped itself around her mouth and spun her around. She felt the firm body of someone behind her, pressing against her.

"Shhhhh," a voice whispered in her ear, their lips barely brushing her lobe. "Be quiet. Don't scream." It was then that she realized that it was Denny. She felt herself relax at the realization. He must have felt her relax too because he let go of her mouth and slid his hand down her arm to grasp her hand. With a gentle tug, he pulled her through the darkness.

"We need to get out of here," Denny whispered. "Something's not right here."

"There is a light over there. Maybe it's a window and we can get out."

"Sure," Denny whispered in agreement, gently tugging her hand and leading her through the dark basement toward the flickering light. As they walked around the last pile of boxes, their worst fears were realized. They were too late. Ricky Osbourne was dead.

Chapter Thirty-Five

He lay naked, stretched out on a table in the middle of the basement floor. Hands bound at his sides, Ricky Osbourne lay on his back, covered in blood. A camp lantern sat next to him, the flame flickering in the darkness of the basement.

"Better call Summers," Tess said as she stepped closer to Ricky's remains. It was then that she saw the true horror in front of her.

Flaying.

Someone—*Brian?*—had started the dark work of flaying Ricky Osbourne, pulling the flesh from his body. Large chunks of skin were missing from both of his thighs, shins, and arms. Fresh cuts along his torso and abdomen still leaked blood from the gaping wounds. His forehead had been flayed off his skull leaving a bloody mess of flesh and gleaming white bone. Tess sighed and closed her eyes in defeat. After a moment, she opened her eyes and looked over at Denny. He looked distraught. As her gaze traveled back up to Ricky she noticed that he had also been emasculated. They were too late to save him in so many ways.

Suddenly, Ricky gasped, his body convulsing as he turned his head toward Tess.

"He's alive!" Tess exclaimed, reaching for him. "Osbourne? Osbourne? Can you hear me? It's Tess." She was only met with a garbled, throaty response from Ricky as his entire body shook. Fresh blood began gushing from the wounds, and Tess pulled off her jacket to help stop the bleeding.

Beside her, she could hear Denny on his phone with dispatch, requesting an ambulance and backup. Focusing her efforts on Ricky, she barely noticed the sound of movement right behind her until it was almost too late. Something metal clattered to the concrete floor and skidded to a stop near Tess's feet: a bloodied knife.

Something was moving behind her. She whirled around in time to see the shadow of someone making their way up the stairs. She yelled Denny's name to get his attention, but he was already in motion. Staying with Ricky, trying to staunch the bleeding, she watched over her shoulder as Denny bounded up the stairs after the intruder.

All of a sudden, the sound of a gunshot filled the basement, a flash of light at the top of the stairs. The slamming of the basement door. She heard a grunt and turned to see Denny falling backwards down the stairs and disappearing into the darkness.

"Denny!" screamed Tess as she drew her service weapon holstered at her side and quickly ran toward the base of the stairs where she found Denny's crumpled form. Through the semi-darkness she could see they were alone now. Crawling over to Denny, she set her gun beside her and leaned over him.

"No! No! Denny!" she pleaded with his prone form. "Stay with me, Denny." She started to panic even as she tried to assess his injuries. "Oh, God." Pulling Denny's phone out of his pocket, fingers slippery with Ricky's blood and now Denny's, she struggled to make the call.

"9-1-1, what is your emergency?"

"This is Deputy Tess Dane. Officer down—make that, two officers down. We need a medic!" She couldn't remember the address. Finally, she just blurted out, "at Deputy Osbourne's home"

"Help is on the way. Is the area secure?"

"Negative. The suspect got away, unsure of the current location."

"Copy."

"Suspect is Brian James Sloane, wanted for questioning in the recent torture murders—should be considered armed and dangerous. He has a gun, most likely Osbourne's!"

"Copy. Responders en route."

Tess hung the phone up to help tend to Denny. Tears slid down her face as she shined the phone's flashlight up and down his limp body, looking for damage. She watched in horror as the hem of his white dress shirt was taken over by an ever-growing red stain.

"Denny. No, Denny," she sobbed, leaning over him. "Please don't leave me here like this." She felt a pulse, strong and steady. A sob of relief escaped her.

"Well, if I knew how much you cared, I would have gotten shot much sooner than this," he said weakly, startling her. Tess gasped as she looked down at him, speechless that he was suddenly alert enough to be making jokes.

"Denny!" Tess said, a hand on either side of his face. "You're okay! I thought you were..." She wiped her eyes, looking down at him.

"You can't get rid of me that easily," he flinched when he tried to move. She gently pushed him down.

"Don't move. You've been shot, whether you feel it or not."

"Oh, I can feel it, all right," he grunted. "Is it bad?"

"I'm not sure. There's a lot of blood." She gently pulled up the hem of his shirt, and near his waistband, just beneath where his bullet proof vest ended, she found a bullet hole. Blood oozed out of it at a rate of speed that alarmed Tess, and she quickly pressed her hand down over it. Denny grunted.

"I'm sorry, Den. I have to try to stop it." Tess said, looking at his face through the murky light of the basement. He reached up then and held her wrist because her hands were occupied.

They stayed like that as the sound of sirens grew louder. Help had arrived.

Chapter Thirty-Six

Wednesday, November 2nd, 1:36 a.m.

The constant beeping of the monitors next to Denny's bed lulled Tess into a fitful sleep. It had been a long night—a long day in fact—and Tess was more than exhausted.

She shifted uncomfortably in the chair she sat in and then woke, groggy and disoriented. Where was she? Oh, yes. The hospital.

Glancing over at Denny, pale and still under his blanket, the emotions of that afternoon came flooding back to her. She'd thought she was going to lose him. Even now, her heart hurt at the thought. Her own response to him getting shot told her more than she was ready to admit to herself, much less to him. She'd always enjoyed his company, always seemed to click with him, but *could there be more?*

She shoved the thought away for the moment and stood. Walking to the window, she pulled back the curtain and looked out at the Columbus skyline. Though it was some time after midnight, the dark night sky was illuminated by millions of lights from the city, casting it in a strange orange-yellow glow.

They still needed to catch Brian Sloane. To put an end to all of the killings and stop the madness. But for now, Denny was safe; and that's what mattered most to Tess. Luckily, he'd been shot through and through, the bullet passing clean through his abdomen and somehow not hitting anything vital. They'd rushed him into surgery and repaired the internal damage as best they could. He was going to be fine.

Ricky Osbourne hadn't been so lucky. He'd died on the way to the hospital, his wounds worse than Tess had determined. Mike Seawell and his forensic team were at the scene now, processing Ricky's basement for any evidence that would tie Brian Sloane to his murder. Surely the knife that Brian had dropped before his escape would prove vital. If only she and Denny had gotten to Ricky's house sooner, they may have been able to save him.

With a sigh, Tess walked back to Denny and paused next to his hospital bed. His closed eyes were twitching as though he was dreaming. The rhythmic rise and fall of his chest told Tess that he was deep asleep. She reached out and lightly brushed the hair from his forehead, his skin cool under her touch.

Suddenly, her phone buzzed as a text came through. Reaching into her pocket to retrieve her phone she read the message.

"536 Maple Street, Crawley. Come alone."

Her pulse quickened. It had to be Brian, but how did he get her number? She quickly typed a response. "Who is this?"

"You know."

"When?" she typed. A pause and then she watched the bubble on her phone as he was typing.

"I'll be here until you get here. Come now," came his response.

"In Columbus. Will take a while to get there. Leaving now." Her fingers hovered over the "send" button. Should she really go alone? Should she tell him she was on her way? She hit the backspace button and then wrote, "Fine." She weighed her options and then made a decision. She hit "send". The less he knew about her whereabouts the better. And she was coming for him. Enough was enough.

Her phone buzzed again, "See you soon."

Chapter Thirty-Seven

Wednesday, November 2nd, 3:00 a.m.

Over an hour later, Tess pulled her vehicle down Maple Street in Crawley, following the directions of her GPS. She'd called the sheriff a few moments ago to let him know where she was so if this all went south at least someone would know where to find her. He'd seemed grumpy and half asleep when he answered. He'd been at the hospital in Columbus with her and Denny until around nine that night before heading back to Camden Town to tell Ricky's family what had happened. Denny was safe, Ricky was dead, and it had taken its toll on all involved. When Tess told him what she was doing, he tried to stop her, telling her he was sending backup.

He wouldn't listen when she told him that she was meant to go alone, which is exactly what she knew he'd do. That is why she had waited, pulled over on Maple Street, just houses down from number 536, and called the sheriff. She was in Crawley, twenty-something minutes from Camden Town. She'd had just enough time to get to the house and confront Brian, alone, as he'd asked. She didn't like it, but she was also over all the bloodshed and torture. She'd almost lost Denny.

Sliding out of her car, she stood and checked her side arm. Her father's old service pistol was tucked safely under the calf of her pant leg. Shutting the car door quietly, she began walking swiftly down the street, when suddenly she heard her father's voice in her head, "*Always be prepared and never leave your duty belt behind.*" Turning around quickly, she made her way back to her car and popped the trunk. Grabbing the belt, she secured it around her waist and then shut the trunk. Adrenaline pulsed through her as she ran quietly over the cracked sidewalks and overgrown yards to the house that Brian had chosen to meet at. Once a nice area to live in, the houses and neighborhood had declined over the past twenty years. It was evident now as Tess made her way past a "For Sale" sign leaning precariously in the overrun yard of 536. The house, once gray with a lion knocker on the red front door, now sat deserted.

Tess glanced around at the neighboring houses and noticed that they were dark for the most part, their occupants tucked in for the night. Carefully climbing the uneven stairs, Tess passed over the sagging front porch to find the front door slightly ajar. Holding her gun at the ready, she gently pushed the door inward. The hinges, unused and rusting with age, groaned in protest. She carefully reached inside the front door, feeling for a light switch. Finding one, she flipped it but it just clicked. Damn it.

Pulling out her flashlight while still holding her gun, she slowly made her way inside the deserted old house. Flashbacks of a few hours ago pulsed through her brain—another deserted house filled with nothing but darkness. Her pulse quickened, breathing fast and shallow. Casting the light around, she found the living room empty with no one lurking in the shadows. She slowly made her way through to the kitchen and bathroom, but they were empty too. Finding the basement door locked, she decided her next choice was to head upstairs.

She made her way to the bottom of the stairs, her footsteps echoing throughout the empty house. Shining her light up the stairs, she saw nothing except some striped wallpaper with a rose design spread across it. Gun in hand, she cautiously made her way upwards, the carpeted stairs muffling her footsteps.

At the top of the stairs was a bathroom, door open, tap dripping. No one was inside. To the left, Tess could see two doorways, each opened to the narrow corridor. To the right of her, two more doors also sat open. She stood there in the darkness of the house, lit only by the streetlights outside and the meager beam of her flashlight. Listening for any sound other than her own breathing, she debated which way to go. Then she heard it: a quiet click. Her head turned in the direction of the sound. Down the hallway to her left, a soft glow from the last room at the end illuminated the darkness. Tess gulped, wishing she'd just stayed at home, tucked under the covers with Otter. But she had to continue. She must finish this.

Steeling her spine, she walked quietly down the hallway toward the light, gun in hand.

"No need to be shy now, Tess," came a deep voice from within. As she approached the doorway, she paused for a second before whipping into the doorframe, gun pointed.

A man sat there, in the middle of the empty room in an old camp chair, a battery operated lantern next to him. He raised his hands and slowly began to clap. A sad smile crossed his face as he watched her for a moment.

"Brian Sloane?" Tess asked, even though she already knew.

"I see you got my package," he said, by way of answer. He looked to be in his late twenties, somewhere between she and Denny. Tess didn't recognize him at all.

"Yes, I did, but not fast enough," she accused.

"To save your fellow brother in blue?" Brian mused. "Honey, it was already too late for that before I even sent the package," he laughed. "That was the whole plan. You were meant to find him when it was too late—except you interrupted my work. I'd only begun to skin the bastard when you and your partner came creeping around. I underestimated the delivery time of the package apparently. Oh well." He gestured to another camp chair, still folded and leaning against the wall in the corner. "Please, have a seat."

Tess quickly glanced at the chair, then back to Brian. He nodded for her to sit.

"If it's alright with you, I'll stand," she said, refusing to take her eyes off the man for another second. Brian made a noncommittal gesture.

"Suite yourself then." A moment passed, each waiting for the other to speak. Finally, Tess broke the silence. One question had burned in her stomach, day and night, since this whole thing began.

"Why me?"

"You mean why did I put your name on the boat? To help you, of course. To move your career along."

"I don't understand," she said, her mind racing. "Help me?"

Brian sighed then, hung his head, and remained quiet for a few moments. She was almost beginning to think he wouldn't answer her when his eyes shot up to hers, moist and mournful.

"Because of your father," he paused again. "He was always kind to my mother, after everything that happened to her. I'm sure you read her diary?" He waited until she nodded. "Even after everyone shunned her, treated her like she was less than human, Tommy Dane was nice to her. He would check on us from time to time. He even brought us groceries a handful of times and paid the electric bill at least twice, that I know of. I didn't know the full importance of your father in our lives until after Mom was gone."

"After reading my mother's diary, I found out the truth. I found out what had happened to her to make her the person she became. She used to be so happy, before everything. But after the attack, a darkness began to grow in her. I am that darkness." Brian stood then, pacing around the room while Tess remained in the doorway.

"She never would tell me who my father was. She would never let down her guard. I noticed that over time, she changed. She fell into a deep depression and eventually turned to drugs, drinking, and prostitution. I remember her telling me once when I was twelve, 'Everybody thinks I'm a whore so maybe I should just be one.'" A tear slid down his face. "My entire life has been a shit storm of poverty and abuse; neglect; feelings of being unloved and an inconvenience."

He paused his pacing, a feeling of anger and desolation pouring off of him. "Do you know how hard it is to find out that your own mother was gang raped and that you are the outcome? That every single time she looked at you she'd remember that night? No wonder she hated me toward the end. Sure, she started out loving and caring, but as realization hit, as the darkness pressed down on her, she snapped," his voice cracked slightly, anguish filling his face.

"Where is she now?" Tess asked cautiously. Brian hung his head, his breathing ragged.

"Dead. She jumped off the old bridge down in Crawley last spring. And it was all their fault."

"Did she leave a note?" Tess asked quietly, her mind racing to remember a comment that Ricky Osbourne had made just a few days ago about the woman who'd jumped to her death from the bridge in Crawley. It had been Brian's mother.

"Yes," he sighed. "She said she couldn't take the nightmares anymore. She'd battled the demons long enough, and she knew those men would never pay for their sins. She had paid enough for their sins, but they hadn't." He began pacing again. "After she committed suicide, I was going through her things. That's when I found the diary."

"But why kill them all so brutally? Why not just bring the diary down to the station and report it?"

"You just don't get it yet," Brian said, stepping closer, his expression of sorrow replaced by anger. "They weren't going to do anything. Your dad tried to report it years ago and nothing happened. As long as the powers that be are still in charge, nothing is going to happen. That's why I did what I did. I got closure for my mother—for myself."

"But why not just emasculate them or shoot them? Was the Blood Eagle really necessary?" Tess asked, understanding why he was upset but at a loss as to why death wasn't enough, that he had to add in torture too.

"The emasculation was to deprive them of their most offending parts. The torture was to make them pay. Sure, I could have just shot them, but that would have been the easy way out for them. My mom had a lifetime of suffering. They only had days. It wasn't enough."

Tess pivoted, readjusting her grip on her Glock. "I still don't understand why you'd pick me to help catch you."

"You see this house?" Brian said, abruptly changing the subject. "Did you know that this was my fake house when I was growing up?" When Tess shook her head, he continued. "My mother would buy me clothes she couldn't afford just so she could take pictures of me out front on the sidewalk. It made people believe we lived here. It was a nice house then, not all run down like it is today. That's why I picked to have you meet me here today. So, I could lay all my sins bare, in the one place my mother loved and wished was hers. I'd buy the place if I could, but I don't have the money. And now that I've hurt so many people, I'm guessing they wouldn't let me live here anyway." He looked up at Tess sadly. "This is the end of the road for me. If I don't get the death penalty, I'm sure I will get life in prison. It'll be worth it though. The truth will finally be known."

She listened intently, a mixture of feelings pulsing through her. She knew how it felt to lose a parent when you needed them most. She understood how it felt to have the other parent not give two shakes about you, and what it felt like when everything was out of your control.

But she also knew that two wrongs don't make a right—that taking the law into your own hands, taking a human life, was the wrong decision. Though she felt sorry for Brian on some level, she knew what she must do.

"I'm sorry, Brian. I really am. I understand part of where you are coming from, but don't you see? In your effort to avenge your mother, you've made three widows. You've taken the fathers of at least four children; five if you count yourself, since technically one of the victims was your father. I know that's not easy to hear, but it's the truth." Tess said, watching as Brian's expression crumbled into agony as he thought about it all. "You can't change your past, but you didn't need to change their future." With that, Brian fell to his knees, a sob bursting from his chest. His body shook as his cries filled the air. He was a man broken.

Tess stood there, watching, giving him a moment before she arrested him. Her mind raced with all the "what ifs" life brought. What if her father hadn't gotten sick and was still able to work? Would she have still become a cop? Would they be working side by side even now? What about her mother? If she hadn't been so selfish, would she still be here with Tess, enjoying the woman she'd grown to be?

Nothing could undo the past. Nothing could bring back Gary Hinsley, Corey Potter, Johnny Carpel and now, Ricky Osbourne. Nothing could bring back Maggie Sloane and erase the nightmare she'd endured all those nights ago.

As Tess stood there, listening to Brian sob uncontrollably, something dawned on her. Something that Brian had said just moments ago.

"Brian?" she said gently, pulling him out of his anguish. He looked up at her, his eyes red and swollen. "Something you said, something about as long as the powers that be are still in charge nothing will happen—what did you mean by that? Who covered up your mother's assault?"

With a mournful look, Brian said, "Bur–" and then his head exploded. The sound of the gunshot thundered through Tess, her ears ringing. Out of reflex, she ducked and pivoted around aiming her gun at the shooter behind her.

Chapter Thirty-Eight

Tess stood there, stunned, watching as the sheriff turned his gun on her. The look of rage and contempt that covered his face as he glared down at her unnerved her.

"Give me that!" he demanded as he ripped her gun from her hands. Shoving it into the pocket of his jacket, he continued to glare at her.

"What the hell!" she exclaimed, slowly taking a step back from the older man in front of her. Sheriff Burrows just continued to glare at her. As she looked at the Glock aimed at her chest, she knew that Brian's last word was "Burrows".

"Go to the living room," the sheriff said, gesturing with the gun. When she stood frozen for a second, he lunged at her, pressing the gun into her temple. "Now."

Tess slowly made her way down the stairs and into the living room, worried about her own safety and wondering what the hell was going on. Brian was dead. There was no way that someone could sustain an injury like that and survive.

"Sit," Burrows demanded, his gaze never leaving her face. He waved the gun in the direction of the floor, and she slid down to do as he'd asked. She stuck her trembling hands in her pockets in an effort to get them to stop. She watched as he walked over to the thick drapes, the only thing left in the empty house, and peeked outside. She was trying desperately to find an escape route, to get back to Denny, but the sheriff stopped her thoughts in their tracks.

"Just stop. You've done enough. And put your hands where I can see them," he growled and Tess pulled her hands out and placed them on her lap. "You couldn't leave well enough alone, could you?"

"Sir, I'm not quite sure I know what you are talking about," Tess said, trying to keep him talking while she formulated a plan. "Where is backup?" she asked, even though she knew now that they would never arrive. "What is going on?"

"They aren't coming... because I never called them," Burrows sneered. "You should have just walked away. You should have just stayed on patrol, writing out speeding tickets to soccer moms in minivans. I never should have allowed Haywood to sweet-talk me into letting you on this case." Glock still trained on her chest, Burrows began to pace. "I've underestimated you, Dane. I should have known you'd be like your father; a good cop, but one that didn't know when to quit."

Tess sat there, fear coursing through her body as she processed his words. "It was you, wasn't it? The one that my father went to, all those years ago. The one that helped sweep this whole mess under the rug?" Slowly her fear was turning to anger, betrayal fresh in her mind. "Why? You're a cop. You're meant to uphold the law, not break it."

"Ha! You think you know everything, sitting over there with your judgmental smugness," Burrows barked a laugh. His eyebrows pinched together. "I was just a patrol officer back then. That's what now... thirty years ago? I was young, married with a baby on the way. I had this kid, Tommy Dane, come barging into the station, going on about some girl that had been attacked. I took down his report. I even interviewed the girl, Maggie Sloane. But suddenly, I was told to cease and desist. Not to utter another word about it. I was threatened, my wife was threatened. What do you think I should have done?"

Burrow began pacing again, his footfalls loud and plodding on the wooden floors of the empty house. "I should have known Tommy Dane would be a problem though. He just wouldn't give up. He kept asking around, coming in to talk to me. And then he moved to Swain county and got a job on the force. But he couldn't do anything about it, except harass me and threaten me with exposure. There was no evidence left at that point; the statements had been destroyed. The statute of limitations expired after twenty years but he got sick before that, so even if he had found some loophole, no one would have believed him. They obviously couldn't ask Maggie anything, even if Tommy had been able to get her to talk to them. She had turned into an addict and suffered from mental illness. Hardly a reliable witness."

"Who made the decision to hide everything?" Tess said, the pieces slowly falling into place. "And if this happened near the school, where everyone attended, then why didn't Columbus PD respond? You were just a small-town beat cop back then." She let her insult linger in the air for a moment.

Burrows didn't seem happy about the barb. "CPD didn't respond, because no one called them." He sighed, almost annoyed at having to explain every minute detail. "The attack *supposedly* occurred at a house in Crawley. The kids at the party had driven the hour or so out here. The only trouble they got in that night was sneaking out of the dorms to go to the party—and the alcohol consumption, of course. But both 'offenses' were ignored, parents in power. You know the drill."

"Who told you to stop looking into it all?"

"It came from up top, the mayor's office," Burrows said. "At first I didn't know all of the names of the boys that were being blamed. When I did, I understood why the mayor wanted everything to go away. I was told that I'd lose my job, my home, even my good standing in the community if I ever uttered a word. So, I said nothing. I even took the samples from the evidence locker when your dad became a cop and began sniffing around."

"Were you paid for your silence?" Tess asked, glaring up at him, "While all the other officers waited to be promoted, get raises, you seemed to rise in rank pretty quickly. I remember my father getting overlooked a few times during his career. He and my mom would be discussing it—discussing how you kept climbing the ladder, but when it was another officer's turn suddenly there wasn't enough funds."

"Despite what you think of me right now, I am a good cop. But yes, my silence did help with moving ahead in my career. Once the mayor died, I thought I was in the clear, that this wouldn't resurface and bite me in the ass. I guess I was wrong." He shoved the gun closer to her. "Everyone else is dead. All my old superiors who might have known what I did, and the mayor. Now it's just you."

"If you knew who was guilty back then, why didn't Ricky Osbourne get fired? He somehow became a member of law enforcement, and you said nothing. Didn't he know that you knew who he was?"

"Oh, he knew," the sheriff retorted. "You see, he's my sister's son. The minute I took the statement from your dad the night of the attack, I knew I'd have to hide Ricky's involvement. He'd always been a fuckup, but he was family. I helped get Ricky his deputy job when he was old enough, so that I could keep an eye on him. I was a corporal for the Swain County Sheriff's Office by that point and put in a good word for him. But, as you know, Ricky was lazy and never really rose in ranks. As I worked my way up the hierarchy, I kept an eye out for him and his mistakes. Once I became county sheriff, I was able to keep up my end of the bargain for good—I wouldn't talk about his past, and he wouldn't talk about my involvement in the cover-up."

"But didn't Osbourne recognize Maggie Sloane out on the streets during his patrol? Surely he recognized her—he made some comment about her committing suicide last spring but didn't seem to recognize her." Tess said, taking it all in while also trying to plan her escape. Burrows paced in between Tess and the window, his gun never wavering from her.

"He claimed he never knew her name, and he only saw her the one time during the attack. Once Maggie started working the streets, she looked so different I don't think he'd remember even if they had been better acquainted." He stopped pacing and stood right in front of Tess, looking down at her. "Are you done playing Twenty Questions yet?" he glowered. "I'm done dealing with all this shit over some crack whore that couldn't keep her pants up."

"That's not who Maggie Sloane was though, Burrows, and you know it," Tess bristled. "She was just a kid, barely sixteen. She got attacked by four boys who were older and much bigger than she was. You could have stopped all of this: the torture killings, the death of your own nephew, the lies. Sure, you didn't cause the assault, but you damn well could have finished it. You are a coward, Burrows. You were spineless and did nothing. This is on you," she seethed. "And now, you are also a murderer."

"I tried to do what I could all those years ago. I just..."

"You did not. You were more worried about your pathetic career advancing to the next pay grade than you were about actually doing your job—upholding the law and protecting the victims of despicable crimes," Tess snapped. The two of them glared at each other for a few drawn out seconds, both full of hate and repulsion at the other.

"Look, you can judge me all you want, but in a matter of minutes, you'll be dead, and I'll be retiring with my pension and dignity intact. Who's to say that Brian Sloane didn't shoot you as you tried to arrest him, and then went and shot himself? You have nothing on me, just your baseless accusations. Where is your proof that any of this even happened?" Burrows laughed.

"I have her diary," Tess said, watching the sheriff's surprised expression as he processed the information. "Oh, and a good crime scene tech would know straight away that the scene was staged. There's no gunshot residue on his hands, no stippling from gun powder on his face. Not to even mention the lack of his fingerprints on the handle of *your* gun," Tess said, her face angry. "That's not even counting–"

"Enough! I am *not* going to prison over this. Do you know what they do to cops in prison?" Burrows roared, anger etched into his reddened face. "I'm tired of your smart mouth. I'm done with all of this. I'm done with you... so we both know what needs to happen now." He raised the Glock level with her face. Just as he was about to pull the trigger, a car door slamming outside distracted him long enough for Tess to react. Within seconds, she yanked her backup gun, her dad's old service pistol, from her leg holster and fired four shots into his chest.

He stared at her in alarm before he looked down at his ever-darkening shirt, the blood spreading quickly. Suddenly he lurched forward and then crumbled to the floor. Tess quickly bounded to her feet, keeping her gun trained on his prone position. She recalled, *The Dead Man's Ten Seconds*—a known rule in self-defense that describes the moment between life and death where the dead man tries to fight back and get the last laugh. *Not on my watch,* she thought as she kicked his gun aside. As he lay there dying, blood seeping into an ever-widening puddle, Tess called for backup—real backup. While the dispatcher took down the information, Tess stuck her trembling hands back in her pocket and sighed. She pulled out the small object hidden there. It was the small digital recorder her dad had given her. She had Brian's, and now Burrows', confessions.

As she checked for Burrows' pulse, she sighed again. He was gone. She'd never shot anyone in her career and as she thought about it, about the fact she'd taken another life, she began shaking. Tears began sliding down her cheeks, even as the sirens began growing louder. She wiped her face and holstered her gun. She knew she'd have to turn it into IA, and answer all their questions. But really, at that moment, all she wanted to do was sleep. It was finally over.

Chapter Thirty-Nine

Denny was released from the hospital a few days later. It was midday when he and Natalie came walking up Tess's front walk as their Uber ride pulled away from the curb. She'd been expecting them. She'd been asleep until about twenty minutes ago when he'd called and asked to come over. After his promise to bring food, Tess flew out of bed and into the shower. Her hair was still damp as she opened the front door for them.

"Hi, Tess!" Natalie squealed, throwing herself at her. Scooping her up, Tess made a grunting sound.

"Ugh! You're getting too big for me! How tall are you now, kiddo?" Tess said, hugging the young girl to her. Natalie just giggled and snuggled closer.

As Denny approached, gingerly carrying some takeout bags, Tess caught his gaze, and her pulse quickened. He watched her expression for a second, and then a huge smile crossed his handsome face.

Suddenly, Otter came bounding out of the house, toy in his mouth, and began dancing at Tess's feet while trying to get to Natalie. Tess sat her down, and the girl took off into the house with the dog, leaving Denny and Tess alone on the porch.

She walked down the stairs to greet him and stopped at the bottom stair. They stood there a second, just looking at each other, neither saying a word. Denny finally moved to the bottom of the stairs, now at eye level with Tess.

"Hey," he said, looking into her face. Her heart was racing. She tried to keep herself busy, afraid that he'd see what she was thinking, feeling.

"Hey back," she grinned despite herself. "Want me to take that?" she said, indicating the bags of food in his hand. He turned and carefully set them on the bottom step next to her. Slowly standing back up, he reached out and took her hands.

"How are you doing? I heard about what happened to Brian and the sheriff," he said, looking into her face for any indication that she wasn't okay.

"Well... I killed my boss," she said, her eyes getting watery. "It can't get much worse than that, right?" She glanced away quickly, then down at her feet, her long damp hair falling into her face. Denny let go of her hand and reached up to push the hair behind her ear.

Tilting her chin up, forcing her to look him in the eye, he said, "You did the right thing, Tess. He would have killed you, just like he killed Brian. Anything to keep his secret buried. He was too worried about his pension and retiring next year. You would have been collateral damage."

Denny pressed his lips into a thin line, looking over her features as he stood there holding her chin in his hand. "He would have killed you, and I don't think I could live with that." His eyes stopped on her lips, and Tess's heart fluttered.

"I felt the same way when you got shot, like my whole life was in slow motion. I didn't know what I'd do if something happened to you," Tess said, reaching up to her face to rest her hand on his. "I'd hate you forever if you left me like that," she teased.

"Does that mean you don't hate me now?" he said, his voice hitching. He swallowed hard, his gaze leaving her mouth and going back to her eyes.

"No," Tess barely whispered. "I don't hate you. Far from it actually."

A grin spread across Denny's face, his eyes twinkling. "It's so nice to hear you say that. And for the record, I don't hate you either. Far from it actually."

He leaned forward and brushed his lips to hers. She leaned into him, wrapping her arms around his neck as he deepened the kiss. A slight moan escaped her throat as his hands slid to her waist, pulling her even closer.

"It's about time," a small voice said from behind them. Tess and Denny pulled apart and found Natalie leaning on a porch post, a huge smile on her face. Denny busted out laughing at her facial expression, and Tess joined in. *Yes, it was about time*, she thought.

Acknowledgements

First, I'd like to thank my parents for always being there, for reading my cheesy stories as a kid, and for letting me just be myself. And Mom, thanks for the many years of homeschooling and all of the English assignments that have helped me become a better writer.

To my sister Megan, thank you for always going along with my silly ideas, for reading my stories even when they are a little too dark for your tastes but being cool enough to give me feedback anyway. You've always supported me no matter what and for that I am grateful. You are my rock, and I love you.

Thank you to Chelsea and Pat for being the supportive push I needed to take a chance on myself. Your positivity and feedback mean more to me than you'll ever know.

To all my friends and coworkers at the animal hospital, thank you for all the support, jokes, questions, and positivity that you've sent my way during all the planning, writing, and publishing to make my dream a reality. You guys make an awesome team and I'm proud to be a part of it.

To Rick Vade Bon Coeur, thank you for being the best forensic teacher a person could have. You took my interest in forensic science to a whole new level. I learned so much from you and your energy made class so much fun. I will never forget making snow casts or hanging out all night for our senior final at The Murder House.

To my editor, Miki, at She Wrights Words, thank you for all the texts, emails, and phone calls during this process. You took the time to answer all of my silly questions and your feedback was appreciated. I hope to become a better writer from all that you have taught me.

Thank you to my friend, Cheryl, for all of your talented artwork in making my cover look amazing! You've been a great friend for so many years and it was amazing having a chance to work with you on this project. You rock, girl!

And lastly, thank you to my partner, Danny and our amazing, smart, sassy girl. Thank you for giving me quiet time to write and collect my thoughts onto paper. The house may have gotten messy here or there but eh... I'll get to it. You never complained when I chose to write instead of adulting. It really means a lot. I love you both, more than you will ever know.

About the Author

A.L. Hatcher holds bachelors degrees in both forensic investigation and forensic pathology as well as an associates degree in veterinary technology. Because of her love of animals, she has been a registered veterinary technician for over twenty years. However, her passion for writing began in childhood when she would write her own short stories and picture books.

Today, she spends her time caring for animals, reading, listening to true crime podcasts, and writing fiction about crime, suspense, and all things dark. She lives in the Midwest with her family, some chickens, and a menagerie of pets.

We'd love to hear from you

If you enjoyed this book, please consider leaving a review on Amazon, Goodreads, or wherever you review books. Reviews help other readers find books that may interest them and also help provide author feedback.

Please feel free to follow the author on Facebook, Instagram, and Tiktok @alhatcherauthor
or sign up for her newsletter at www.alhatcherauthor.com

Email: alhatcherauthor@gmail.com

A.L. Hatcher is currently hard at work on the second Tess Dane Thriller, coming 2024.